CENTERLINE

CENTERLINE

by PETE TRUDGEON

Dot Screen Studios

Book design and illustration by
Mike Ortiz

Published by Dot Screen Studios.

ISBN: 978-0692378939

For Mike:
Who tolerates me.

"Out of the Past into the future."
~ *Centerline city motto*

"When you feel that you have right on your side, you can do some pretty horrific things."
~ *Weather Underground member Brian Flanagan*

ONE

POSTED ON BMIVALENTINE.COM ON 12-15-13
BY DEAN LIRIOUS

PIN-UP FAV VALENTINE USHER SETTLES IN THE LINE

What's up, just your boy Deano here. Well, it's been nearly a year since our fav girl, U.S.O. pin-up Valentine Usher was honorably discharged back into civilian life. Immediately afterward she went off grid and what many of us assumed to be the quiet life of self-imposed retirement.

But take heart my fellow Valentine admirers cause 'ol Dean here has it on good authority, thanks to my sources in all the right places, that our fav girl has just been approved for residency in the munitions district located in Centerline, Michigan. It seems our gal Val spent some time in the wilderness, you know what they say about Detroit, it's where the weak are killed and eaten, and that goes for the two as well as the four legged. Life under the dome will surely seem like paradise.

Our lovely Miss Usher isn't remaining idle she's joined the roster of exotic dancers at an establishment called 'Stray Katz' (meow!) where she'll be a featured performer. It seems all these prayers offered to see our fav girl in her birthday suit have finally been answered.

Yours truly has been hard at work to hook you all up with a video stream. So stay tuned cause in the very near future you'll be able to thrill to Valentine in the buff and in action.

TWO

Cal had given it considerable thought, him and Valentine, and he always came to the same conclusion, that their sleeping together had been inevitable. All those years filled with glances that lingered just a second too long, simultaneous reaches for the same object and not so accidental brushes of one body against another. They'd come so close to the cliff only to step back at the last second. Then came the night, they'd been in the Line for six months, Cal had come home and found Valentine watching television in her underwear. Like the saying goes, one thing led to another. When he awoke the next morning Cal's scalp was sore from Valentine's impassioned hair tugging, his back was a map of cat scratches and his neck sported a pair of hickies.

For a long time Cal had believed Valentine would never let a man touch her again. They'd spent nearly four months in the wilderness while on their way to the Line. He'd left her alone so he could search for water. It'd been a stupid thing to do, but Cal thought he'd be gone for only a few minutes. Besides she had a piece and knew how to use it and someone had to guard the car, the same one they scraped the day they reached the Line.

Who knows how long that wolf pack had been watching them, just waiting for the opportunity. Valentine had the urge to pee so before she dropped and squatted she'd set her gun down on the hood of the car. That's when they jumped her, although they didn't anticipate what a wildcat fighter she was. The one wearing the leather vest was about to penetrate her when Cal returned, his AK ready to cut them all in half. But he only lined them up, angel-faced Valentine who capped them, all three.

The youngest, a little shit who couldn't have been a day over twelve balled like a baby while he pleaded for his life. But Valentine had ice water coursing through her veins; she put two in his head, just like she'd done the others. Cal figured that experience would've flipped her to lezzie, except she never put much trust in either gender.

Two weeks later they finally reached the Line. They had their info processed, passed the physical and were cleared through security. First thing they did was hit a store so they could buy a six pack. They drank it in the parking lot, then sold that piece of shit car and checked into a motel. The next morning Cal had to go to police headquarters. He'd spent three years in the Middle East, it helped him cinch the cop gig and the ride on the gravy train began.

THREE

Before the war Centerline was a speck on a map, a city measuring only 1.7 square miles and resting inside the bigger suburbs of Warren like a dog turd on the sidewalk. Originally an enormous swamp, it'd been drained and cleared by a combination of French, German, Belgium and Irish immigrants and settled in 1837. It'd been those same French who named it Centerline because it was the middle of three Indian trails running from Fort Detroit to the northern trading posts. Nearly a hundred years later it was incorporated as a city, filled with auto workers, mostly shit kickers who'd migrated from the south.

But when the war started the first year of Obama's second term, well, everything changed. Most of Europe had flushed itself down the toilet, whole parts of England and France were Muslim territory where even cops feared to tread. America was circling the bowl, the lucky few were hoarding while the rest ate cat food, or the cat itself. Chicago, Cleveland and Detroit had to burn before the president finally admitted to being a mere mortal, but he was still mindful of his legacy so he started going to church, a lot. All those prayers must have worked cause sweet Jesus handed him a gift by having San Francisco nuked.

The government always claimed they didn't know who was responsible; it could've been North Korea, Iran, or Martians. Of course the conspiracy buffs thought it was an inside job while religious types said it was God's will, the smiting of the modern day Sodom and Gomorrah. Eventually the president, along with the majority of the country blamed the Middle East as a whole, we never trusted those oil peddling, rug kissers anyway.

4

Frisco getting wiped off the map was the prelude for the domino fall. They finally put up the damn fence, massive deportations began, many who worshipped Allah didn't wait to be asked to leave. Obama discovered his inner hawk and plunged America into the biggest war since WWII sporting a blue steel hard-on. Lefties all across the country ranted, raved and sobbed like a collection of jilted lovers. Everyone knew the game was rigged, but it was the only game in town.

Valentine had just gotten out of her cap and gown then told high school to go fuck itself. Cal had barely tasted his first beer of the summer when the draft was reinstated. Twelve weeks later he was shipped off to Libya. On the way over some asshole said, "Don't worry, this shit will be over by Christmas," and jinxed the entire world.

While Cal was dodging bullets Valentine decided to join the U.S.O., she was quickly assigned to the newly created V-Girl department where she, along with dozens of other young women, travelled across the country for war bond drives and troop send offs. Many noticed the girls outfits were barely there, but it was for the boys so few disapproved aloud.

Valentine caught the eye of a higher up who decided her magic would be one hell of a morale booster. One photo shoot later and the resulting photos of Valentine in a stars and stripes bikini could be found in every soldier's barracks, including Cal's. It soon after gained a place on many a teenage boy's bedroom wall.

Centerline had been expanded, rezoned into a munitions district. Eminent Domain was used to relocate most of its eight thousand residents although a handful of local businesses were allowed to stay. The entire city was sealed under a dome made of charged plasma; inside an electrified fence was added for extra security.

Due to the nature of the weapons produced plant workers were rigorously screened, when someone signed up for a job in the Line it was for the long haul, three years minimum. The only way out was in a coffin or an end to the war. Workers were on a rotating schedule, four days on, three off. Down time was devoted to recreation aided by genetically engineered marijuana and alcohol that gave the buzz without the side effects.

The media that was allowed in was carefully screened for maximum patriotic effect, America; the last best example of liberty would triumph, eventually. But the war was rarely a topic of concern for the population of the Line. Compared to what was going on outside and overseas life in the Line was sweet, and being a cop was the sweetest. What you said went and fuck 'em if they couldn't take a joke. Not that there was much crime to fight, the occasional brawl, the busting up of a still of home brew. Sometimes a good 'ol boy would get some of that white lightning in him and make a run for the fence, but for the most part things were peaceful. So, while most of the world scratched its eyes out, Cal and Valentine had never had it better.

FOUR

POSTED ON BMIVALENTINE.COM ON 1-20-14
BY DEAN LIRIOUS
VALENTINE'S STREAMING DEBUT: HOTTIE TOTTIE
HEALTHCARE

Finally, the wait is over. 'Ol Deano offers a thousand apologies, turns out I had a few more palms to grease then I'd originally thought. But I'd decided long ago at the start of this venture that duckets were no object. So, to all of you out there who doubted the Dean's power, look no further except to check out our premiere presentation. A Valentine to all you Valentine devotees.

Stray Katz is run by the regal Miss Lila Dean (no relation to the Deano) who prefers her girls to use the old school theatrical touches, real all-American Burly-Q, complete with a theme for the day. Our fav girl takes the stage dressed as the naughtiest nurse you've ever laid eyes on, who knew white could be so wicked. Check out that bitchin' bob cut and dig them candy stripes. I don't need a thermometer to know I'm running a fever.

FIVE

Valentine had chosen Stray Katz because of its name. Half the clubs that lined the main drag called Van Dyke had kitschy names, The Treasure Chest, All-Girls School, and Teasers were just a few examples. She'd also liked the sign that hung above the front entrance, spelled out in pink neon, the "S" and "K" in bold capitals while the remaining letters were written in cursive. There was a figure, a Betty Page look-a-like dressed in a leopard print bikini, cat ears and tail, posed so she was using the "S" as a scratching post.

The Club's owner Lila Dean was both stern as a nun and gentle as a grandmother depending on the situation. She'd worked in burlesque back in the day when a stripper could gain status of national fame. Lila had known them all: Lily St. Scar, Tempest Storm, both women's autographed eight by tens were behind silver frames and hung on her office wall. They shared space with the other ladies, Lila's own wall of fame.

She wore her silver hair in a tastefully teased Jackie O. bouffant, favored floor length gowns, mink wraps and diamonds dangled from her ears, encircled her thin neck and winked at you from eight of her ten fingers. Valentine's audition was simple and brief, it consisted of going to Lila's office where she was asked to strip down then Lila gave her a visual once over. She was pleased that Valentine's body was tattoo free.

"They're not lady like," she remarked.

Valentine had never had the desire to get one, besides U.S.O. V-Girls weren't allowed to have them. After she got dressed Valentine improvised some moves to 'In My House' by the Mary Jane Girls for about a minute. After she turned off the

8

music Lila gave Valentine a satisfied smile.

"You'll do well here Miss Usher. But always remember, you're a professional, I won't tolerate any lewd behavior on-stage. So, my dear, when can you start?"

Cal had fronted her some cash so Valentine could buy herself a new look. First, she had her hair cut into an above-the-shoulder bob, then had the stylist put in some blood red streaks, which complemented her natural raven color. The rest of the money went for some outfits. Cal was able to stick around for part of Valentine's first shift. She could tell he liked what he was seeing and it reignited the flame inside her. She made enough to pay him back, in full, within a matter of days.

Valentine could've made twice as much of the long green if she'd gone into flat backing. It was legal in the Line; the typical split with the house was forty-sixty. The brothels were clean and except for the security detail they were entirely owned and operated by women, madams who took even less shit than the cops. Rape was a death penalty offense, there was no worry of pregnancy or STDs, everyone in the Line got a twice yearly shot, a combination of contraception and anti-viral. Not that anyone came to the Line to raise a family. So, for Valentine working at Stray Katz was logical, she had the moves and had been born with a stripper's name.

SIX

July, outside the Line Michigan was getting baked, Detroit would be like Hell with the lights on, at night was when the shit would get really hairy. But under the dome the environment was kept at a comfortable 72 degrees year round. Cal lay in bed watching the shadows of tree branches as the swayed across the ceiling. As she was in the habit of doing at least three days a week Valentine had woken Cal by climbing atop him and initiating a morning quickie. Immediately after orgasm she'd dismount and light up a post coital joint.

Cal turned his head to take in the sight of her, skin lightly damp with sweat, her ruby navel ring refracting sun light. She exhaled a final thin curl of purple smoke before she snuffed out the roach in a heavy crystal ashtray.

"How long before rye bread arrives?" she asked.
It was the nickname of Cal's partner Ryan Nader. The guy was a bit of an asshole, a fact he was completely aware of. Nobody remembered who'd bestowed the sobriquet, but it'd stuck, like gum on the bottom of a shoe, although no one used it to Ryan's face.

Cal checked the bedside clock. It told him it was three minutes after seven a.m.

"About an hour," he said.

"Want something to eat before you go?"

"No thanks."

Valentine began to rub his leg with her foot, something that

10

always inspired a new erection. But then the sound of Cal's cell phone blaring 'You got Another Thing Coming' by Judas Priest took his attention. It was Ryan's ring tone and the man rarely called this early. Cal picked up the phone, hit the video option on the touch screen.

'Yeah."

Ryan's face filled the screen. "Get some clothes on, I'm outside."

The screen went black. Even in one sentence Cal could hear the agitation in his partner's voice, but despite Ryan's distress Cal still took time to shower, dress and plant a goodbye kiss on Valentine.

Ryan had parked their cruiser in front of Cal's house, he leaned against the reinforce hull inhaling from a one-hitter. Cal wasn't a pot smoker, he knew more than a few badges who used on-duty. He didn't disapprove; the engineered stuff didn't dumb a person down. Still, he found himself wishing Ryan would exercise some discretion.

"There's been a break," he announced.

It was supposed to be impossible to break into a munitions district. There had been a handful of attempts, all unsuccessful. "Are you sure?"

Ryan vigorously rubbed his shaved head.

"A sewer tunnel, one older than Zeus' balls, DPW is claiming it doesn't show up on any of the rezoning maps. Captain Tyson is on scene and was expecting us fifteen minutes ago."

Without another word Ryan got in the driver's side.

Before entering the cruiser Cal turned and saw Valentine in the door way. She blew him a kiss and disappeared back inside.

SEVEN

The drive to the breach site took less than five minutes, Ryan remained tense, the pot hadn't seemed to have helped his mood, he kept glancing at Cal apparently waiting for a reaction to the news. But Cal remained silent; he wasn't going to make an assessment until he had all the facts.

"You're taking this calmly, do you understand what this means?" Ryan asked.

Cal lit a cigarette. "We finally have to start working for a living."

"Why do you always have to be so fucking cute? All it takes is one successful hit on a plant and all those pukes will get inspired."

Ryan had a tendency to forecast the worst possible outcome.

"That's not going to happen because we're not going to let it. Bypassing plant security is a whole lot more difficult than crawling out of a hole. Besides, for all intents and purposes this is a small town, unfamiliar faces tend to stick out."

"What if it's an inside job? For all we know they've been coming and going for months and it's just dumb luck we found out."

It was something Cal hadn't considered, but he chose not to vocalize it. He turned his attention to the shield, which glowed a coral pink in the morning sun. When their cruiser arrived at the intersection of Sherwood and Rinker they saw a half dozen other police vehicles already parked at the curb. Ryan found a

13

space in front of an empty lot that'd once been a trailer park. Standing fifty yards ahead was a small cluster of badges standing in a circle, cigarettes dangling, cups of coffee tipping, all were staring at the same spot.

At six foot four Captain Ellis Tyson stood out. Barrel chested but muscular, his thinning straw blonde hair combed back. He had narrow eyes and a hooked nose that gave him the look of a pissed off gargoyle. He caught sight of Cal and Ryan and jerked his chin up in greeting. The other badges muttered their hellos. Every time he saw the captain Cal always took a second to notice his superior's night stick. Unlike the retractable graphite model carried by Cal and the others Tyson's was made of oak and handmade. He'd inherited it from his father, a Detroit cop who'd had a beat in the nineteen 60s and 70s. Amongst select company the captain would share stories of the skulls his old man cracked during the '67 riots.
"What do we got captain?" Ryan asked, as if I wasn't obvious. The manhole cover, which at some point had been paved over lay inches for the perfectly round hole in the ground.

Captain Tyson let out a snort. "Troubles what we got, this tunnel goes almost three miles into old Warren. That sides been resealed, bomb squads already been through, no booby traps which means they had future plans for it."

Cal glanced down the hole, nothing but a black void. "Is the DPW still claiming ignorance?" he asked.

Tyson hocked up and spit in the hole. "Yeah, but it seems for once they're telling the bible truth. Not that it matters, we're the ones who are going to have to track down these sons a bitches."

The captain's attention was taken by the arrival of a DPW truck, a never washed white, six wheeled monster that farted exhaust and stank of diesel. When the driver jumped down from the cab Tyson was there to greet him. Cal couldn't hear what was said, but judging by the way the DPW man's head was bobbing up and down it was a real lashing, Tyson thought public works was nothing but a collection of gold bricks. After he finished the dressing down Tyson ordered everyone back to headquarters, they were getting a call from Natalie Coulter, director of the anti-sedition forces.

EIGHT

The Centerline police force was housed in the Michael Smith building, named after the city's first top cop, but everyone called it the cathedral. With its glass and steel spires that rose toward heaven, not to mention the formidable shadow it cast, it looked like a place of worship and fear. It reminded Cal of something out of 'Logan's Run,' an old movie he'd seen on the box. The design was no accident, it was meant to remind everyone in the Line that America was a Christian nation, despite what the seculars thought, and she was at war with foreign heathens.

Practicing Islam wasn't illegal, just inconvenient. Muslims weren't allowed in or within five miles of a munitions zone. Although never officially blamed for the Frisco bombing the cloud of suspicion stuck like snot. When they began leaving the country in significant numbers the district grew, along with the good riddance's.

Cal and Ryan slipped through the sliding doors of shatter-proof glass and into the ground floor lobby. A pair of green, jump-suited maintenance workers were operating mechanical buffers that polished a floor already clean enough to eat off of. On the wall above the reception desk hung the CPD seal, a bald eagle against a stars and stripes background, a scroll clutched in its talons read 'In Defense of the Homeland.' They joined a hand-ful of officers in an elevator, the doors opened on the third floor where the strategy room was located. The stadium-style seating made it look like a college classroom, except instead of a black-board there was a 20x50 video screen. To the right of it was a podium where Captain Tyson stood watching the men file in.

After Cal and the others were seated the lights dimmed while on the video screen the emblem of the Federal Office of the Anti-

Sedition Forces appeared. It faded into the image of the affairs director Natalie Coulter. Forty-two years of age, but looked like a co-ed, her long blonde hair cascaded over her shoulders, her glacial blue eyes had a gaze so focused Cal wondered if it could snap spines. She didn't tolerate criticism of her office, or cops in general. Left-leaning talk shows had stopped inviting her out of fear of the verbal beat downs she dished out. If you were law she had your back, it bought her fierce loyalty.

"Greetings, gentleman," she said in a tone that was school teacher seasoned with a dash of affection.

"Earlier today my office was informed of the breach of your security. It is my unfortunate duty to tell you yours was not an isolated incident. Our intel points to this as a coordinated action carried out by a combination of the Red Brigade and New Weather Underground. Until now both groups have kept their activities within the realm of lawful protest. It would seem their tactics have taken a turn towards the violence of the past.

As you are all too well aware this is no ordinary conflict we're engaged in. Although, much of the media are loathe to admit it, we are in the midst of a holy crusade, a fight for the very soul of our beloved country and the Judeo-Christian principles on which it founded upon. By their unlawful entry into multiple munitions zones they have demonstrated their contempt for our country. Their intent is nothing less than sabotage and thus denying us the ability to defend our country against her enemies. They have voluntarily surrendered their rights under the Constitution and been found guilty of treason.

Your job is clear, locate and apprehend these terrorists. Use of deadly force is authorized, extreme prejudice gentlemen. May god bless you and god bless the United States of America."

NINE

Valentine leaned against the wall smoking her mid-shift joint. Lila didn't like her girls stinking up the dressing room so if anyone wanted to light up they had to come out to the alley. She tabulated, her bank account had gained weight, men were always ready and willing to donate to the Valentine Usher retirement fund. News of the security breach had wild-fired through the Line and the other dancers were flapping lips the minute Valentine returned to the dressing room. Everyone knew she was shacked up with a badge so they thought she might have a few extra tidbits, but were soon disappointed, she knew what they did.

The mood of the customers had an anxious taint. Cal had always told her that munitions plants were immune from sabotage, not even cops were allowed in without a security check. But Valentine could tell people were stepping up on their blowing off of steam. Coincidentally, it was military day, time to boost patriotism by peeling down to that all-American nakedness. Valentine's uniform of choice was black, complete with a visored cap and knee-high boots. If anyone thought she resembled a kinked out Gestapo officer they kept it to themselves. Besides, black was the sexiest color. Valentine had quickly ascended the rank amongst the dancers, and she maintained, customers took pride in their allegiance to a particular club, the die-hards inked it on their skin. Valentine knew of a few forearms that had her name unfurling across a black and red heart.

It sure as shit beat life in the U.S.O. where too many of the girls were catty to a fault and had dreams that were bigger than their talent level. Those years were mostly a blur of high school gyms, V.F.W. halls and countless hours on a bus, the ceaseless panorama out the window, fields and one cow after another.

Valentine had never realized how much of America was empty space. Then there was the wilderness, which she wished she could forget.

The weed was making her mildly horny, a side effect the engineers had left in. Many of the other dancers were switch hitters, but Valentine was a one-man woman and not into girls, so she'd have to keep it in check until Cal came home. She couldn't help smiling to herself. The notion of her and Cal being together had once been impossible to imagine and it filled her with a wicked glee. The world would be damned, it probably was already.

Valentine snuffed out the roach, popped it in her mouth and chased it with peppermint breath spray. On her way in she ran into Tawny and Sapphire, the three exchanged a friendly hello. If there was any envy between the dancers it was never displayed. Lila didn't tolerate any bullshit, if you had a problem bitch at home to your man, or quit. Valentine glided over to the DJ booth where Bugsy was spinning. He was a cherubic black man who kept his head shaved and his gentle green eyes that looked at you from behind gold frames. A true gentle giant who's benign nature had been mistaken as weakness by a few customers. They got their faces pounded into hamburger. He smiled when he saw her.

"Hey Valentine, is there something special I can play for you?'

"Yeah, for my next turn I'd like some Vanity 6."

"You're an old-school kinda girl, for which I thank my lord and savior."

19

Valentine had always had a preference for vintage songs. 'Nasty Girl' never failed to get the money flowing. She looked forward to the fresh contributions to the Valentine Usher retirement fund.

TEN

It was nearly eight in the morning when Ryan finally dropped Cal off in front of his house. It'd been a rag-ass day, he stood on the front lawn and lit a cigarette so his bad mood would dissipate. Cal had wanted to know more about who he might be dealing with so he downloaded the basic facts about the Weather Underground Organization. Founded in Ann Arbor on the campus of the University of Michigan their stated goal was the creation of a classless society, world communism. Bernardine Dohrn and Bill Ayers were on top of the shit heap. One of the WU's first stunts was called 'The Days of Rage,' essentially a riot held in Chicago in the fall of 1969. Unfortunately for them the cops came prepared; they were well-trained and armed. Many WU members got their asses kicked, six were shot and half of them were arrested. The WU ended up shilling out $243,000 to bail out their comrades.

Between '69 and '75 they carried out a series of bombings, most notably at the Capitol building and the Pentagon. In 1970 Dohrn had made the big time and was placed on the F.B.I.s most wanted while ten of the thirteen WU leaders had outstanding warrants. But due to the bureaus fuck ups the charges were dropped. By '77 the WU had disbanded.

They'd come back during the first months of the war, but hadn't done much but hold some protest marches, they weren't taken seriously. That changed on January 20, 2012 when Bill Ayers was killed when an explosive device planted in his car was detonated, both man and auto were virtually disintegrated. Conspiracy theorists' money was on the C.I.A. Whomever was responsible gave Bernardine Dohrn an excuse to return to her bad habits.

So where the fuck were they? Sure Centerline had grown during the war, but the expansion had barely been an additional
mile. Cal and Ryan had spent the entire day burning gas and
chasing ghosts. Cal smoked the cigarette down to the filter then
tossed the butt into the gutter and headed inside. He'd been
given six hours off, just enough time for a meal, a lay, and
few hours of shut eye. Inside the house Curtis Mayfield was
singing 'Freddie's Dead,' Valentine only seemed to like music
recorded before she was born.

She was at the rear of the house sitting on the couch and watching the muted television. Her damp hair was combed back, her
naked body was wrapped in a black and red kimono, without
makeup she looked like a teenager. When she noticed Cal in
the doorway Valentine jumped to her feet and into his arms. As
she kissed him he felt slightly embarrassed, he reeked of smoke
and frustration while Valentine smelled of jasmine bath oil.

She sat Cal down, shut the radio off then went into the kitchen,
returning with three opened beers, one for her, the other two
for him. Valentine could always read his moods, Cal accepted
the beers, "Do I look that bad?" he asked.

"You look tired and thirsty," she said as she sat down beside
him. They didn't resume speaking until Cal polished off his
first bottle. Valentine jump started, "Streisand made good on
her promise, she left for Paris this morning."
International travel was a dodgy business since the beginning
of the war, but as they always had celebrities operated under a
pretense of elitism.

"Any chance her plane crashed in the drink?"

"Nope, landed safe and sound."

Valentine draped one of her bare legs over Cal's, he reflexively massaged it, it felt warm and baby soft.

"Are you hungry?" she asked.

"No." He wasn't, despite not having eaten all day.

"How serious is it?"

"We got a pep talk from Director Coulter."

"Then it's true, about the break-in?"

"Yeah, turns out we weren't the only ones. But we haven't found jack shit and I have to be back on duty by two.'

"It was in the air, the way guys were throwing money around, there was something desperate about it. Could someone really break into a munitions plant?"

"Hasn't happened yet, hasn't stopped a few from trying."

"I don't know what scares some of the girls more, the possibility of a terrorist attack or potential loss of income."

"They're not going to shut down the main drag just yet, for now it's business as usual. But until this is over and done with I want you packing your heat."

Valentine nodded, she picked up the remote and flipped over to a movie. They watched in silence as Cal finished his second beer. When the bottle had been emptied she turned to him. "Baby, let's go to bed," she said.

ELEVEN

Valentine was awoken by the explosion, it'd been close enough to shake the house. She'd heard glass breaking, when she looked over at Cal he already had his pants on. After putting on a tee-shirt and boots he strapped on his gun then told Valentine to stay put, she didn't get a chance to reply. After Cal left Valentine got onto the bed, but all she could see were the houses across the street. The chorus of car alarms was soon joined by the sounds of sirens and the voices of the people who'd come out of their homes.

Valentine felt a slight chill, realizing she was naked she pulled the sheet off the bed and wrapped it around herself. She looked down at the floor, fragments of glass were sprinkled around the dresser. A picture frame had been knocked off, it contained a photo of her and Cal taken their second week in the Line. She hoped it wasn't an omen.

Valentine threw the sheet back on the bed, put on her kimono, and headed to the kitchen where Cal kept a fifth of Jim Beam in the cupboard. Neither of them were whiskey drinkers, the bottle had been a gift, from who she couldn't remember. Even though the seal was broken the bottle was still almost completely full. Valentine poured two fingers worth into a glass. The first swallow burned going down, but after a couple more sips she felt the warmth growing through her body and she finally started to relax.

She thought she should be doing something, maybe turn on the TV and see if there's any special instructions. Then, a darker thought intruded, "What if this had been done in order to draw Cal and other officers into an ambush.

"Come on Valentine, you need to chill out. Cal will be okay," she said to herself.

Valentine had always been only mildly religious , she'd never seen any concrete proof for or against the existence of God, but she found herself doing something she hadn't done since elementary school. She began to pray.

TWELVE

Cal stood staring at a smoldering crater that was as wide as a two-car garage. He'd ran the three blocks to Manner Park, a mostly unused patch of green. Despite the fact there were no children in the Line no one had thought to dismantle the wooden jungle gym that sat at the northern end. All around him were half-dressed civilians who'd been donkey punched out of bed by the explosion. A few men, obvious bachelors stood with cans of beer clutched in their hands, looking irritated that their drunk had been interrupted. Others went about shutting off their wailing car alarms and complaining to no one in particular about their blown out windows and how they had to be at work in a couple of hours.

Amazing, Cal thought, how people could complain instead of being glad to be alive and not blown to splinters like the trees that had been closest to ground zero. The ones that hadn't been erased from existence were burning like dried out Christmas trees. As far as Cal could tell no one had yet showed up with a bag of marshmallow.

The fire trucks and police cruisers had announced themselves by blaring their sirens and flashing their lights. Cal witnessed half a dozen near collisions between vehicles and humans. As firefighters pulled out hoses and searched for hydrants cops moved the crowd back. Cal recognized some of his fellow officers, but decided not to acknowledge himself, he didn't want a taste of the grief they were starting to receive. There was nothing for him to do so Cal decided to head back home.

A hole that big had taken a significant amount of explosions, why did they waste it blowing up a chunk of sod? All the files he'd read on the WU had left him with the opinion they were nothing more than a collection of sanctimonious posers, and their allegiance with Islamists didn't make sense, they seemed to fail to realize that as atheists their Muslim buddies would slit their throats the second the opportunity presented itself.

As Cal neared his home it seemed things had finally began to settle down, only a handful of people loitered on their porches having a cigarette. Some nodded or waved when they saw him and he returned the greeting.

When Cal entered the house he heard music, then he spotted the bottle of whiskey on the kitchen counter and realized how badly Valentine had been spooked. He followed the tune to the bedroom, there was Valentine in her kimono and slippers sweeping pieces of glass into a dust pan while 'Little Latin Lupe Lu' came out of the bedside radio. After she deposited the bits into the waste basket they embraced, when Valentine kissed him Cal tasted the heavy sweetness of the whiskey.

"How are you feeling?" he asked as he stroked her hair.

"Okay, the booze helped. Rye bread called while you were out, he said he'd be right over."

Five minutes later as he was about to walk out the door Valentine again wrapped her arms around him.

"Be careful. I love you."

"I will. I love you, too."

Neither of them had a habit of vocal pronouncements of affection, so on these rare occurrences they came with a touch of anxiety.

Cal didn't protest when Ryan wanted to drive by the crime scene. The fires had been extinguished, the area blocked off and only a few civilians still milled about. Ryan stopped the cruiser just long enough for a glance before stepping on the gas and heading for the cathedral.

THIRTEEN

After her traditional greeting followed by a brief introduction Director Coulter's image segued into a recorded video message. It was delivered by a woman who appeared to be sitting in a dimly lit basement. Her hair was limp and grey, her face was cracked by age. But her eyes were alive, still burning with indignant rage. Bernardin Dohrn was 76 years old and looked every minute of it, but when she opened her mouth she sounded identical to her self-righteous sixties incarnation, every word dripping with bile.

"This is a communique from the Weather Underground to the imperialist government of America. As should already be clear to you we have infiltrated the very heart of your genocidal war apparatus, which in collusion with the Zionist forces of Israel that has murdered tens of thousands in an illegal war against the oppressed peoples of the world.

Tonight's action was just a small taste of the fear you've been inflicting for years, it's also the only mercy you can expect. The hour of your destruction has arrived, let the slaughter of the pigs begin. All power to the people, death to the fascist insect who preys upon the people."

Dohrn concluded by giving the upraised fist salute.

The strategy room's video monitor went black for a moment before Director Coulter's image reappeared. Cal wondered if the woman actually slept. While some of the other badges were still rubbing their eyes and stifling yawns, she appeared as fresh as Dohrn had looked haggard. As she addressed the men one could hear the usual confidence in her voice.

"Our psych department has been studying this as well as her other communications. Their conclusion is that Miss Dohrn's mental state has been in a steady decline. She has grown increasingly paranoid, only engaging in personal contact with a very small group of close confidants. Also due to her advanced years it's believed she is suffering from a number of physical ailments. It is strongly possible that she may not be making the actual decisions for the WU, but instead merely acting as a figurehead. Still she's managed to evade capture, but only temporarily. We will apprehend her and she will get all that is coming to her."

Director Coulter's image shifted to the left side of the screen, beside her appeared a map of the northern United States; red dots marked the areas hit by the Weather Underground.

"Despite the low casualty rate blood has been drawn. The size of these explosions points to the possibility of help from sleeper cells inside your borders. So I'm issuing the following direction, until such time every Weather Underground agent has been apprehended all citizens living in an armament zone will be required to carry their Eminent Crisis I.D. on their person at all times. They must be prepared to produce it upon request by law enforcement officers. Failure to do so will result in immediate arrest and the possible deportation to a penal colony. Step up your efforts gentlemen, remain vigilant, in the end we will prevail. May God bless you and God bless the United States of America."

After the director signed off Cal could feel the change in the air, she had succeeded in firing the men up. Captain Tyson let the buzz in the room run for a minute before he called for order.

"All right, listen up. You all heard the director, now hear me. You see anyone on the street between dusk and dawn who doesn't seem to have a purpose or destination you stop them. No ECID, smack them down hard. If the shit gets thick shoot first. Remember, watch each other's backs, keep your safeties off and aim for the head. That's all, dismissed."

As they stepped off the elevator Cal heard his stomach growl. He remembered he hadn't eaten since the previous day, he suggested to Ryan they swing by Kunrods Corner a diner that was favored by badges. While they were stopped at the intersection of Sherwood and Ten Mile Ryan turned to Cal, "You know back in the 1800s this entire area was once considered an impassable swamp. People detoured around it, miles out of their way. Because it was infested with snakes," he said.

"That your way of saying history is repeating itself?"

"History is nothing but a snake eating its own tail."

FOURTEEN

"That was some bit of trouble last night," the cab driver said.

"Yeah, it sure was," Valentine replied. She was always slightly amazed at the euphemisms people employed. A brain rattling explosion set off by terrorists had been reduced to a term usually reserved for an overly loud party.

"Where to, Miss?" asked the cabbie.

"Stray Katz, please."

"I thought you looked like an entertainer."

Valentine had done as Cal had asked, she was carrying the Beretta he bought her during their first weeks in the Line. Cal had set up a target range in the basement, they made a point to practice regularly. She'd gone from a fair shot to pretty darn good. But this was the first time she'd worn a shoulder holster, the way it dug into her side was an annoying distraction. The cab dropped her off in front of the club, Valentine went to the employees entrance at the side of the building. After swiping her worker's I.D. one of three she was now required to carry, the door opened.

Inside the dressing room the other dancers were in full sewing circle mode. Before she even set her purse down Valentine was intercepted by Karla, a bleach blonde with just-capped teeth.

"Did you hear the bomb go off?" she asked excitedly.

"Yes, it woke me up."

Who in the Line didn't hear the damn explosion, Valentine thought. Her response seemed to satisfy Karla who fluttered away. Valentine sate down at her station, set her purse down and turned on the lights that circled her mirror. The gun jabbed her side again so she slipped her jacket off.

"Oh shit, ladies, look out Valentine's packing," announced Iris, a carmel-skinned amazon who's hair extensions went down to her rear end.

Each dancer at Katz had a locker on the right side of their dressing table which was opened by thumb print identification. Valentine opened hers then stashed her gun. That done, she began getting changed. It was faerie tale day, Valentine's first choice of the day was Little Red Riding Hood. She'd just finished zipping up her red thigh highs when she spotted Tanya, the new girl, eighteen and fresh off the bus. She was from some small upper-peninsula town nobody had heard of. Country cute with shoulder length blonde hair and blue eyes that still had a little girl in the big city wideness.

Tanya had been with the club only three months and her dancing was still somewhat awkward, but many of the customers seemed to find it endearing. Valentine wondered if her lack of polish was intentional, and if so more power to her, whatever it took to pull in the green. She noticed Tanya was the only girl who seemed outwardly anxious, but chalked it up to her youth, which was accented by her Little Bo Peep outfit complete with a small stuffed toy sheep.

Valentine returned her attention back to her own costume, putting on the red hood and short cape that was held on by a small clasp. She heard Tanya receive her thirty second curtain call. Valentine was three dancers down the roll call so she decided to watch Tanya's performance to see if she could determine once and for all if her clumsiness was genuine or not.

After Tanya stepped onstage Valentine positioned herself off to the side behind the curtain. It was immediately apparent something was off, Tanya's movements were stiff, even for her, and the expression on her face was one of distraction. The audience didn't seem to notice, or if they did they didn't care. Valentine's eyes fell upon a couple seated in the second row center table. Boyfriends and girlfriends came to the club all the time, but she didn't recognize this pair, plus neither seemed to be enjoying themselves. They stared straight ahead, even in the dim lighting Valentine could discern the disdain in the woman's face.

Had Tanya caught sight of the pair, in particular the woman's sour expression, and was it affecting her performance? One of the first things Valentine learned was how to ignore the occasional dour customer, usually men who showed up in a bad mood and were unable to shake it. Tanya had seemed already stressed out backstage and these two were making it worse. It wouldn't take long for their shitty mood to spread. Valentine had seen it happen, it would fuck up every dancer's stage time, hers included. Tanya had made it down to her g-string and boots, her toy sheep still clutched in her hand. All of a sudden she froze in her place, Valentine thought she'd been psyched out. She was about to go out and help her off stage when Tanya raised the toy animal over her head.

"Death to the fascist insect that preys on the people!" she shouted before giving the toy sheep's tail a sharp tug. Purple smoke began pouring out of it, she threw it into the audience and the smoke cloud expanded with surprising speed. Then the woman who'd been staring Tanya down tossed her something. It seemed to fly through the air in slow motion. It was a pistol that appeared to have been modified.

"Oh shit," Valentine heard herself say. She turned and beelined back to the dressing room. As she ran passed the other dancers she could hear the sound of gunfire mixed with the shouts and screams of the club's patrons. Valentine made it to her locker, opened it, retrieved her own gun and clicked off the safety. The other girls had been stampeding out the back entrance, rearranging the furniture as they went.

Valentine had a hunch Tanya would try and make her escape through the same rear exit so she hid behind one of the turned-over make-up tables. She didn't have to wait long. Tanya entered the room spraying it with bullets from a machine gun pistol. The shots flew over Valentine's head and into the wall, it bought Tanya enough time to dash out the exit.

Valentine made the decision to follow, she got to her feet and charged through the door, it made a sharp racket as metal slammed against brick and she got into a crouched position. Tanya spun around, when she pulled the trigger of her gun nothing happened, she'd used the last of her ammunition shooting up the dressing room.

"Fuck!" she spat out before tossing the weapon. Tanya turned to retreat, but she only made it a few steps when Valentine fired her own gun, the bullet hit Tanya in her left calf. Her mostly nude body was pitched forward hitting the ground sounding like a slab of meat. As Valentine approached her Tanya managed to flip over to her back, she looked like a broken doll, one of her elbows had gotten badly scraped and blood was trickling from her lower lip that had already begun to swell.

"Looks like your dancing days are over," Valentine said. She could hear sirens in the background. Tanya glared up at her. "Fuck you, bitch. You allow yourself to be objectified for money. You're worse than those males you perform for." Her indignation made Valentine grin.

"You, drop the weapon!"

Valentine looked up and saw a young officer, his sidearm pointed at her. She calmly and slowly placed her Beretta on the ground and with her hands raised, she stepped away from it. The badge kept his gun trained on her as he approached, holstering it before placing handcuffs on her. He placed a call for backup, seconds later two more officers arrived, one, the oldest of the three paused when his eyes spotted Valentine.

"Rookie, uncuff this young lady," he said.

"Excuse me lieutenant?"

"Just do it, then call a meat wagon."

After the bracelets were removed the man introduced himself.

"Name's Hoffman, Miss Usher, we met last Christmas."

He held out his hand, she shook it and apologized for not remembering. He grinned, "That's okay, I got a forgettable face," he said flashing a wink.

"Not to worry, Miss Usher, you're not under arrest, but I'll still need you to make a statement."

"Of course, I understand."

"Just follow me, you two keep an eye on this one 'til the wagon arrives."

"Yes, sir," they replied in unison.

Valentine followed the lieutenant out of the alley. "We'll have to hold onto your gun for a short spell, just a formality, you'll get it back within 24 hours. Nice shot by the way." He gave her another wink.

"Thanks," she said with a smile.

FIFTEEN

Cal was half way through his cheeseburger when the call came over the cruiser's radio, shots fired at 'Stray Katz' gentlemen's club. Ryan nearly broadsided a delivery truck as their car tore out of the diner's parking lot. When the cruiser came to a halt outside the club they found the place swarming with police and EMTs. Cal and Ryan exited the car, Cal immediately surveyed the scene, it didn't take long for him to find Valentine, she was the only Red Riding hood in the crowd. Some of the other dancers had planted themselves curbside, smoking and chatting amongst themselves.

Valentine was leaning against a police cruiser calmly speaking to a lieutenant Cal recognized, his name was Hoffman.

"Hey, babe," Valentine chirped when she saw Cal.
"Are you all right?"

"Not a scratch."

Without having to prompt him Hoffman began filling Cal in.

"Nine fatalities so far, a bunch were injured while fleeing the building."

"How many shooters?"

"Three. Miss Usher here tagged one of them in the leg."

"No shit?"

"Nope, she's getting patched up on her way to the cathedral for interrogation."

"What about the other two?"

"Over there." Hoffman pointed his thumb towards a blue Chevy van that had run into a lamp post. "Driver died on impact, the passenger shot himself in the head."

"If she's all done, I'd like to take her home."

"Sure thing, I've got everything I need."

Ryan had quietly joined them. "Tyson's called a meeting. Why don't you take the car, I'll hitch a ride and meet up with you back at headquarters."

Cal gently took Valentine by the arm and led her to the cruiser. He opened the passenger door and helped her get in.

SIXTEEN

Valentine and Cal spent the brief drive home in silence. She liked the way he seemed unaware of his consideration of her, she was the only one who saw his softer side. When she asked him to come inside he was resistant at first, but when Valentine wanted him she wasn't about to take no for an answer. Something about the day's violence had excited her, once behind closed doors she pawed at him like a horny teenager. Within seconds she had him down on the couch. Valentine cornered Cal into these quickies whenever possible, there was a frankness to these brief, concentrated exercises in sexual gratification, and she was aware he liked submitting to her control.

After Cal had left Valentine stripped off the remainder of her clothing, leaving a trail that ended at the entrance to the bathroom. While the tub filled with hot water she went into the kitchen, retrieved the bottle of whiskey and poured two fingers worth over ice. Valentine felt a strong urge to make the world fuzzy around the edges.

She sat the glass on the edge of the tub then slowly lowered herself into the water, sliding down until her chin was hovering above the surface, her feet propped under the tap. Valentine took a sip from her drink, the ice cubes had melted enough to soften the burn. She took another swallow and decided to wait until the ice was almost completely liquefied before taking another. Valentine soon felt completely relaxed, the post-shooting adrenaline had been worked off. Shit was upside down, Cal was the one who was expected to get shot at. Still, she was lucky to have him. Being a badge's girl, one was spared certain inconveniences. Her statement would be the end of her involvement. If any more was needed from her Cal would take care of it, she wouldn't even have to go to the cathedral.

Valentine knew the club would be closed for a few days, a loss of income but a welcomed vacation. She looked over at her glass and saw that the ice cubes had almost completely melted. After a generous swallow she wiggled her toes and felt inebriation give its first caress.

SEVENTEEN

Tanya's real name was Rebecca Ann Swain of Grosse Point, Michigan. Her father Donald had been an executive at Chrysler while her mother Marion busied herself with various charities. Before the war they were liberal democrats of the cocktail party variety.

Rebecca had been born with the proverbial silver spoon, life for her was one of pampered shelter. She'd left for the University of Michigan a year before the fighting broke out, when she returned for the Christmas break she refused to even acknowledge the holiday. At parties Mr. Swain often joked about giving Rebecca a DNA test because he wasn't sure the young woman under his roof was the same one he'd sent off, then he'd laugh. He was, after all, just joking.

But behind the smile Donald Swain wasn't joking. He didn't recognize this girl. He'd threatened to cut her off financially but it had no effect. Rebecca didn't seem to care about money. She'd spent that week reminding her parents they were oppressors of the people, although she never got into specifics. She came off as self-righteous, sanctimonious and rehearsed. Much of her disdain was held for the shield the Points had installed six months after the bombing of San Francisco along with the hiring of a private security force. Both had been implemented after the remaining citizenry of Detroit had endured months of deprivation and finally coming to the realization that the President they elected wasn't going to save them, they'd decided to storm the temporary barricades.

Cal had heard about it while he was overseas. It'd been ugly, the people from Detroit hadn't taken into account that the Points had been preparing for just such an event, something they'd considered inevitable. Nor did they know what efficient killers the paid security forces were, or how much they wanted to engage someone, anyone.

The points may have been part of the state of Michigan, which was part of the United States of America, but in the controlled chaos the rules had changed. No one said it aloud, but everyone saw it. Sometime during the attempted invasion, some referred to it as a rebellion, it all depended on where your sympathies lay, Rebecca vanished. At first her parents assumed she'd returned to Ann Arbor. Instead, she went off the grid, bought a new identity and made her way to the Line. Her credentials weren't forgeries, something of interest not only to the Centerline P.D. but to the anti-sedition forces as well.

Rebecca had been taken to the cathedral, which had its own dispensary. Her wound was cleaned ad dressed, but she'd been denied pain killers, which made her belligerent. Her attitude changed when she was taken to see Dr. Bela Lorre, the head of intelligence extraction.

The betting pools had sprung up before Rebecca had crossed the cathedral's threshold. Cal and Ryan sat in their cruiser waiting for the next update, Ryan had two bills on her spilling in under thirty minutes. The shooting had gone down at approximately 2:30, it was nearly quarter to four when the news was broadcast that Rebecca had opened like a book. Ryan was two hundred bucks poorer.

"The little bitch held out for almost an hour, you think Lorre's losing his touch?"

Cal lit a cigarette. "He kills them with kindness, some take longer to slay than others."

They were interrupted by the shrill chirping of the cruiser's video monitor which automatically switched itself on when an important message was about to be transmitted. Captain Tyson's face appeared on the screen, cropped at the top and bottom he looked meaner than usual. "All units return to headquarters and rally at tactics. Hope your gear is I order 'cause we're going on a field trip."

The screen went black, Cal and Ryan exchanged a look of apprehension.

"I think I'll give Valentine a call," Cal said, taking out his cell phone. But Valentine never answered, instead it rang half a dozen times before finally going to voice mail. Cal decided not to leave a message.

EIGHTEEN

Valentine had dozed off on the couch under the blue light of the television. She roused herself reflexively stretching and curling her toes until the knuckles cracked. As she rubbed the sleep from here eyes Valentine saw that the sun had begun to set. Her gaze went to the TV screen, it took her a few seconds to realize it wasn't a war movie that was playing, but a newscast.

The police were engaged in a shoot-out. Valentine recognized the location, it was the Engelmann an apartment complex for low income city workers. It stood two stories high and took up an entire square block. She thought it was the most mundane structure she'd ever seen and couldn't tell which side she was looking at. Half the windows were spitting out Halloween orange flames and sooty, black smoke.

Valentine had muted the sound, but she could still read the ticker that ran across the screen. The Weather Underground were said to be inside, they'd refused to surrender and opened fire. She knew this was being broadcast for more than the voyeuristic spectacle, the government wanted to show the people of the Line that the business of law and order was being taken care of. People in munitions zones were well paid, well fed and entertained as such they weren't candidates for conversion by a bunch of leftists. The WU had so far made a big hole in the ground and shot up a strip club. If there was a method to this madness it was too vague for Valentine to perceive.

She checked her phone, Cal had called, but didn't leave a message. She knew he was somewhere in the fray, but all the cops were dressed identically in black body armor and wore gas masks, so trying to look for him would have been pointless.

Her favorite pipe, a ceramic smiling Buddha, glazed an egg white was resting on the coffee table. She'd packed it before she dozed off. She found a disposable lighter, but just as she was about to light up Valentine thought she'd caught movement out of the corner of her eye. She set the pipe down and pricked up her ears. Sure enough she could hear the sound of something skulking around the rear of the house. Valentine stood up, cat-like her bare feet padded across the wood floor. She reached the bedroom, stored in the closet was Cal's pump action shotgun, already loaded.

NINETEEN

Cal, Ryan and a half dozen other officers had managed to make their way to the east side of the Engelmann. It looked out at an empty field of dry grass, behind the electric fence the plasma shield was shimmering a pale rose red. They'd taken cover behind the six foot high cinder block wall that surrounded the complex's dumpsters. Most of the men had slipped their gas masks over their faces to avoid the stench.

The Weather Underground had given the residents a chance to leave. They'd exited as instructed, hands over their heads, and after a once-over, straight into one of the waiting containment vehicles. It'd been mostly half-dressed men, judging from their faces, they'd been enjoying a sound sleep. The second the doors of the trucks were closed the bullets began to fly. It quickly became apparent that these supposed revolutionaries couldn't shoot for shit. So far, the most serious injury suffered was a twisted ankle acquired by an officer while diving for cover. Cal heard someone over the radio, using a tone of mock horror that 'The bastards had just killed a Stop sign.'

Everyone shared a chuckle before Captain Tyson's voice came over the air ordering everyone to 'cut the shit and keep the line clear.'

Ryan had stacked some plastic milk crates so he could peer over the top of the wall.

"Cal, take a look at this," he said. Cal joined him on the makeshift pedestal. A man in his early twenties had run out of the building. He wore nothing but a pair of jeans and was running at top speed across the field. Cal and Ryan watched in silence as the man went straight into the electrified fence where he was fried instantly.

"Fuck me!" Ryan exclaimed. "What was it, fear, or was he so zooted he thought he could make it over?"

Cal shrugged. "Maybe he thought it was a better fate than life in a penal colony."

Just then the order came through their headsets. "Green to proceed, repeat, green to proceed into the building to conduct a sweep and clear."

TWENTY

Valentine had retrieved the shotgun, it was a pump action model that held six rounds and fitted with an attachment that carried an additional half dozen shells. She racked it as quietly as she could while she tip-toed towards the rear of the house. Valentine didn't have much experience handling such a weapon, something she made a promise to rectify in the future.

If it was a person lurking outside it was a stupid one. Thievery was almost completely unheard of in the Line. Occasionally a good 'ol boy would cook up some white lightning, steal a car and go for a joy ride, but it was a rare occurrence.

Valentine crept back towards the kitchen, she crouched against the wall and peeked around the corner. Directly across from her was the door that led out onto the backyard deck. She considered grabbing the phone and texting police H.Q. when she heard the click that signaled the lock had been bypassed. Several long moments passed before she heard the door slowly open followed by a few cautious footsteps. Valentine swung around the corner with the gun held at chest level.

The intruder she found herself facing was a young man barely out of his teens. His long, brown curly hair partially obscured his eyes. He looked like he'd tried to grow a beard, but the facial hair had sprouted in uneven patches and did nothing to hide his adolescent appearance. Valentine took notice of the forty-five that was tucked into the waist band of his olive drab khakis.

They stared at each other in silence, his expression was one she'd seen before, that of someone who's just realized he's gotten in over his head.

"Hands up," she commanded. He obeyed.

"Are you alone?" she asked.
He nodded, but Valentine didn't believe him. Her suspicion was confirmed seconds later by the sight of a shadow that darted behind the boy who attempted to use the momentary distraction to draw his gun. But Valentine's reflexes were quicker, she pulled the shotgun's trigger, the blast hit him full bore in the chest. He flew backward, his body crashed through the screen door and landing on the wooden deck with a resounding thud.

Next came the sound of squealing tires, whoever was behind the wheel cared more about escaping the scene than the fate of their comrade. Valentine lay the gun down on the kitchen counter, before she called it in, she wanted to see if she could find a clue to the boy's identity. Technically she'd be tampering with a crime scene. But since it appeared she was the intended victim she felt justified.

Valentine found a pair of rubber gloves under the sink and slipped them on. Taking care not to step in the blood that had begun to pool around the body Valentine gingerly reached into the back pocket of the boy's pants and found his wallet. After she extracted it Valentine stepped back into the kitchen so she could examine its contents. There wasn't much, a twenty dollar bill, which went straight into the pocket of her kimono. He had a standard I.D. card, it said his name was Brad Stieger. It looked genuine, but the fact that he didn't possess an E.C.I.D. meant it was just a very good forgery. She slid it back into the wallet. Valentine found one more item, a photograph. When she turned it over she got a slight shiver up her spine. It showed Brad sitting on a rock, a broad grin on his face. Seated on his lap was Tanya a.k.a. Rebecca. She was also smiling, but it looked forced.

TWENTY-ONE

When Cal finally emerged from the Engelmann it was still burning, the fire crews didn't want to risk any of their own while shots were being fired. Now, with shooting having subsided they got to work extinguishing the flames. He leaned against a cruiser, removed his helmet, gas mask, and took in a lungful of air. It stunk of smoke and synthetic fabric. Cal dug out his cigarettes, while he smoked he tried to recall how many people he'd shot. It'd been a turkey shoot, a blur of faces, mostly angry, others piss-pants scared. Bernardin Dohrn had gathered a group of naïve kids, taken advantage of their natural inclination to rebel, stoked it white hot and finally set them against a force they had zero chance of defeating.

Maybe creating anarchy was the point. Perhaps the WU leadership knew infiltrating the Line was a fool's errand, but satisfying their own passions was what was important now if it meant some would be sacrificed.

As Cal tossed the butt away he saw Ryan and Captain Tyson approaching. The Captain was poker faced, Ryan, as usual, failed to hide the fact that something had happened. Tyson got right to the point. Valentine was at the cathedral, someone had broken into their home, she'd shot and killed the intruder.

"Don't worry, she's uninjured, but from the details I've gotten it seems the perp was Swain's boyfriend."

"How the hell did he find out she was the one who tagged the Swain bitch, and how did he find out where we lived?"

"Lorre's got her in his chair and she'll spill. It's in her best interest to cooperate," Tyson said. He turned around and left to

51

attend to other matters.

When Cal arrived at the cathedral he was informed by one of the desk sergeants that Valentine had been taken to Captain Tyson's office. He found her there stretched out on the couch sleeping. She looked so serene he felt a little guilty about waking her. When he gently nudged her Valentine's eyes opened. She set up and gave him a gentle kiss on the lips.

"I'm glad you're all right, they showed the shoot-out on the TV."

"How are you doing?"

"What can I say, you know how much I dislike unannounced guests," she said with a grin.

Cal wasn't surprised by her casual attitude, this Stieger kid wasn't the first Valentine had shot and killed.

"Don't be pissed, but I checked the guy's wallet, I saw the photo of him with Rebecca."

"I'm not, is there anything else?"

"He had twenty bucks on him. I took it, asshole tax."

"You're a piece of work," he said planting a kiss on her forehead. "Let's go home."

Cal had wanted to question the Swain girl, but he was told that Dr. Lorre had finally consented to giving her pain killers. She was off in dream land, Cal wished her nightmares.

On the way home hunger came roaring for both of them so they stopped at a 24-hour deli where they ordered a couple of Reubens. They ate their sandwiches in the car. When they finally made it home Valentine found herself in an ambivalent mood. Only a few hours had passed since the love-sick Brad Stieger had tried to turn her lights out and while the connection to Tanya/ Rebecca was disturbing she refused to let it overwhelm her thoughts. She was glad the evidence techs had cleaned the place up, they even installed a new door with a better lock.

Cal was exhausted so Valentine helped him undress, then put him under the shower so he could wash the day away. He fell asleep the second his head hit the pillow. Valentine kissed his cheek before she headed back to the TV room where the Buddha was still resting on the coffee table. She'd needed to get stoned before her mood began to dampen. Her and Cal's life in the Line had been easy-peasy, and they'd fucking deserved it after all the shit they went through in the wilderness.

Valentine fired up and took a deep hit off the pipe. She didn't think about the past much, especially in the pre-war years, she didn't like to. But she found it hard not to considering recent events.

While Cal had been overseas she'd been surviving, better than many, but life in the U.S.O. had never threatened to make her rich. Sure she'd received offers from big wigs to be a mistress, after her discharge a porn producer offered her twenty grand to do a single scene. A career in modelling could have been a way to go. She may have chosen one of those options had she not fallen in love with Cal.

Valentine had always loved him, but his physical absence had ignited something deeper. It was during Cal's first weeks back stateside that she first began to feel the temptation to seduce him. But she resisted it, not only afraid of rejection, but also of Cal's revulsion.

Their time in the wilderness was a life where you never let your guard down, not even while asleep. Once they'd finally made it to the Line and settled in Valentine's desire was allowed to return. There were occasions where she thought she'd seen glimmers of encouragement, but she could never be completely sure. Then came the night Cal returned from a party given for some graduating cadets. Valentine made the first move. Cal offered no resistance. Over-night their relationship had undergone transmutation. Valentine took a final hit from the Buddha. She exhaled smoke rings while staring at the cloud above her she felt the sudden desire to hear some music. As 'Dreamboat Annie' played out of her iPod Valentine entertained thoughts of life on the outside. There were still a lot of cities that were dangerous, but she's heard it was relatively safe in the south. Valentine sould love to have a place on the water where she'd live in her bathing suit. Cal and her would sleep 'til noon, cook outdoors, get stoned and screw like minks. No, she couldn't indulge in these kinds of fantasies. Valentine pretty much ignored news of what went on outside the dome because she didn't care. For all she knew the wilderness had gotten bigger. She shut off the iPod and joined Cal in bed, snuggling up close and putting her ear against his back. Valentine fell asleep to his heartbeat.

TWENTY-TWO

When Cal awoke the next morning he felt fortified, cooking smells floated into the bedroom. After he called Ryan to let him know when to expect him, he went to the kitchen where Valentine was busy fixing breakfast. Cal gave her a peck on the cheek, poured himself some coffee and sat down at the table. He paused momentarily to glance at the new door the evidence techs had installed. It was made of some new material, strong as steel, and coated with a finish that made it look like wood. It appeared real if one didn't look to long. Neither of them spoke of the previous day's events while they ate their bacon and eggs. They'd been through worse.

Cal walked out his front door with a singular ambition, to question Rebecca Swain. On the drive to Ryan's he phoned Dr. Lorre who informed Cal she had awoken from her narcotic-induced slumber.

Ryan took over behind the wheel as Cal could read the file he'd downloaded on Bradley Stieger a.k.a. Brad Steiner, born 9-4-98 to William and Caroline Steiner, a pediatrician and family lawyer respectively. Though raised on the upper west side of Manhattan young Brad attended the University of Berkley. In his second year came the first signs he was playing footsy with radical politics. Until then Brad led a comfortable if unremarkable life. Then he suddenly dropped out of Berkley and ceased communication with his parents. It happened around the same time Rebecca Swain pulled her own disappearing act. Eventually, their two paths crossed. Brad fell in love, who knew what, if anything Rebecca felt for the dead boy.

*

Rebecca Swain was being held in the fourth floor detention area, cell twelve. Dr. Bela Lorre stood outside, he greeted Cal with a handshake. He was a short man standing at an even five feet and round. He reminded Cal of a beach ball in a lab coat. He wore his jet black hair slicked back and it shined like patent leather. Lorre's face was a portrait of benevolence, he always spoke in the same soft and reassured tone. This gentle demeanor disarmed people, they instantly trusted him and found it difficult to withhold information. No one really knew of his life outside the walls of the cathedral.

He immediately began to fill Cal in, "She gave the location of her comrades quite readily. I believe she'd been instructed to do so. It's also my belief that the skirmish at the Engelmann was meant to be a diversion."

"A diversion from what?"

"I don't believe she knows, Miss Swain was most likely only entrusted with a limited amount of information. Captain Tyson has authorized your questioning of her. Please keep any physical distress below the neck. Now, if you'll excuse me I haven't yet had my breakfast and I'm rather famished. Have a pleasant day officer."

Cal watched Lorre nimbly make his way to the elevators, he didn't know if the below the neck remark was sincere or the doctor's idea of a joke. He turned and slid his police I.D. through the card reader and was buzzed into a windowless room that was lit by fluorescents. Rebecca 's left wrist was cuffed to her hospital bed. She was dressed in a white, one-piece gown and appeared to have been bathed. The lack of make-up made her look junior high young. When she saw Cal she fixed him with a scowl.

"Can I get some more painkillers? My leg is fucking killing me."
'I'm not a doctor," Cal said as he flipped through a copy of Brad's autopsy report. He found the boy's morgue photo.

"Congratulations, Becky, thanks to you a lot of people are dead."

He placed the photo on her lap.

"Including your boyfriend."

Cal saw the brief, subtle flash of shock on Rebecca's face before she turned the photo over. Her expression returned to its original look of contempt.

"Nobody calls me Becky. I loved Brad as a comrade, but he wasn't my boyfriend. He just couldn't completely rid himself of his bourgeois ideas about male/ female relationships."

Rebecca was a parrot of the first order, but spouting of the party line made Cal grin.

"Looks as if Brad was more old-fashioned than you thought.; he broke into the home of the woman who shot you. I suspect to avenge you, he got killed for his trouble. I didn't know the Weatherman approved of personal vendettas."

"They don't, a waste of time. Like I said, Brad had out moded ideas. He was always giving me these love poems filled with childish, sentimental notions. It really bothered him that I'd been picked to work at that club. That woman who shot me, what's her name, Valentine, I take it the two of you are lovers."

"We're a lot more."

"Good for you."

"Her home is my home."

"If Brad knew Valentine was shacking up with you and still went through with it, then he was a bigger fool than I thought."

"How'd he find out where we lived?"

"How should I know?"

"Think hard."

"You're a cop, so you know information is just another commodity, it has a price. For all I know one night I got stoned and went on about what a Queen Bee I thought she was and he took it upon himself to follow her home."

"I believe you. Why was Stray Katz targeted?"

Rebecca emitted an exasperated sigh. "I already told all this to that doctor."

"Now tell me, or no more meds."

"You'd do that?"

Cal didn't respond, he let his stare do the talking." It was Fran Zishn's idea. She's Red Brigade, said any woman who allowed themselves to be objectified for money were traitors to their gender. She chose the club at random."

"It seems your agendas are all over the place."

Rebecca lay back and stared up at the ceiling, "I always thought coming here was a stupid idea, like we ever stood a chance of getting into one of those plants. But who the fuck was going to listen to me. So, what's gonna happen to me, am I gonna be executed?"

"Penal colony most likely. Your family has been notified, no doubt they're pulling favors. A word of advice Becky, start searching your memory, if you have any useful information I suggest you give it up."

"Betray my comrades."

"Might get you sent somewhere with a temperate climate."

*

As Cal rode the elevator to the ground floor lobby his anger returned. Rebecca Swain was just another naïve girl who'd swallowed an ideological pill, had allowed it to subvert her personality and was going to piss away the next few decades behind walls. When she reached the penal colony she'd better cozy up to the toughest dyke she could find, otherwise she wouldn't last long. Rebecca was right about Brad. He got himself killed because he'd loved a woman who didn't care about him.

Lorre had offered the idea that the Engelmann shootout had been a diversion, but from what? If the Weather Underground had some grand scheme they were running out of time to implement it.

TWENTY-THREE

POSTED ON BMYVALENTINE.COM ON 7-17-15
BY DEAN LIRIOUS
HOLY KOMMIE KILLER!

Just when 'ol Deano didn't think things in the Line could get any krazier, it turns out our fav girl really knows how to dish out a healthy serving of buckshot.

My sources have told me that the members of the Weather Underground have managed to, in their best thief-in-the-night mode, sneaked into the Line as well as several other munitions zones. These knuckleheads made some noise by setting off several boom booms, all in public parks.

They successfully snuffed out many a capitalist gangster squirrel.

Then to our shock and awe their next act of freedom fighting was to shoot up our beloved 'Stray Katz.' But fear not, our fav girl escaped unscathed, and even managed to squeeze in some patriotic duty by busting a cap in one of the offending Reds. Three cheers for our all-American girl.

Speaking of Reds the Dean has it on good authority that this incident was not even an officially sanctioned WU boondoggle. Nope, seems our favorite gang of ball busting bulls the Red Grigade had a bee in their birkenstocks. They just couldn't stand seeing ladies workin' hard for their money, and as a result 'Stray Katz' has been temporarily closed for repairs.

My sources have also informed me that things took a turn for the personal. Our fav girl's home sweet home was broken into, the perp was armed and his intentions for the lovely Valentine were of the no good variety.

Except.

Our valiant Valentine got the one up on this dastardly deed doer, giving him a killer's kiss courtesy of her handy dandy scatter gun, so not only is the divine Miss V keeping the Line beautiful, she's also keepin' it clean. God bless our all-American girl.

Meanwhile the WU retains its title of World's most inept terrorist organization. Congrats, chumps.

TWENTY-FOUR

Valentine had just gotten off the phone with Lila Dean, she'd called to let her know of 'Stray Katz' reopening which would be in two days. All of the dancers were returning, except for Sabrina who'd taken a bullet in her arm. While Valentine was glad she'd soon be back on the job she was slightly bummed over the end of her idle time. Cal's shift wouldn't be over for a few hours, there wasn't really anything to do around the house so she decided to go for a walk and clear her head. Valentine changed into a violet tee shirt and a pair of jeans, then stuffed her I.D. cards into her back pocket. Although she'd gotten her Beretta back and considered bringing it along she'd decided to leave it at home.

She took a few hits from the Buddha before walking out of the house, the synth dope made colors more vivid. Valentine stepped off the porch, looking both ways down the block she saw no one else was out. At this time of day that wasn't unusual, people were either at work or home sleeping until shift change.

Valentine decided to head for the park, she'd avoided it since the bombing and was curious to see how far along the way the restoration was progressing. She went east on Chalmers then took a right on Memphis, the only other living creatures she saw were a pair of squirrels. They chased one another across several front lawns before darting up a tree. They were a common sight in the Line, it was birds that you rarely saw. Her mother had kept a pair of finches, Valentine remembered how they nervously hopped from one perch to another, the way they pecked at their seed dish and how long it took to clean their cage. While in the wilderness Valentine had seen crows, sparrows, robins, seagulls and others, but in all her time in the Line she'd only seen a pair of pigeons and a single blue jay.

Valentine wondered where her parents were, it'd been four years since she'd last saw them. Both had been devout church goers who believed the bombing of San Francisco had been a sign of coming times. When they told Valentine of their plans to move north, all the way to Soo St. Marie at the border with Canada, she instantly knew there was no way she would join them. Cal had already left for basic training, Valentine didn't want to join a combat unit so she opted for the U.S.O. At seventeen she didn't need her parents' permission and once her signature was on the dotted line there was nothing they could do. The night before her swearing in she packed a bag and took off. Valentine hadn't left a note, it was a decision she regretted.

Three months passed before she tried to contact them only to find their phone had been disconnected. She'd rarely thought of them since her arrival in the Line. Had she wanted to, it probably would've been easy to locate them. Cal was a cop and former military so he had access to various data bases, but she never put forth any effort. Her parents were part of the outside world, she knew it existed, but it remained out've sight, so out of mind. It was the same world she'd been pondering a return to, now she was beginning to have doubts.

As she neared the park Valentine grew increasingly curious about how much damage had been done, but it was quickly apparent that it was an unremarkable scene. There were about two dozen DPW workers at work, some laying fresh strips of sod over the area where the crater had been while others planted trees. Soon only the memory of the incident would remain, the attitude expected of the Line's populace was business as usual.

As Valentine's eyes continued to take in the scene they fixed on a children's jungle gym at the opposite end of the park. Constructed of greenish grey wood it was practically hidden by overgrown brush. It was simple in its design, consisting of a slide, monkey bars, a pair of swings and a two-tiered platform, a lone reminder of the pre-war Centerline where children had lived and played.

Valentine was struck by the realization that while she often noticed the absence of animal life she barely ever thought of the non-existence of kids. It probably was the result of the bi-annual shots she and everyone else received, which retained libido while eliminating the desire to procreate. Not that she ever had a strong maternal instinct to begin with. Valentine liked kids well enough, as a teenager she'd done plenty of babysitting, but had never entertained the notion of having any of her own.

As Valentine entered the park she decided to walk along its outer edges so she wouldn't be in the way, if any of the workers noticed her presence none of them acknowledged it. She neared the jungle gym, smelled the scent of the freshly laid grass and listened to the hum of men's voices that mixed with the mechanical noises of their machines.

Despite the fact that the park was rarely used, even by nearby residents, it was well maintained by the DPW. So it was a bit odd at first to see this tiny area in slight neglect. Perhaps it was intentional, to keep away any unwanted nostalgia.

Valentine was able to easily make her way through the waist high overgrowth. She found the step ladder at the rear of what was basically an observation tower about fifteen feet high, she quickly sealed it and hoisted herself onto the top. As she leaned over the railing Valentine was surprised that such a minor elevation improved her vantage point and it lent the park's expanse a touching quality. When things calmed down she'd bring Cal here for a picnic.

Valentine looked over to her left as two DPW workers approached, they reminded her of Laurel and Hardy. It was soon apparent they hadn't noticed her. The stout one seemed irritated and was venting to his thin colleague.

"They keep shoveling the same horseshit, telling me it's nothing, just a glitch, since it's not my department I should just shut up. These computer jockeys are a bunch of smug pricks. But I got a buddy who services those things, he told me it's a lot easier to disable them than they let on ..."

Valentine had remained unnoticed as they passed directly under her and went on their way. She remained on the platform for several more minutes before climbing down and heading home. During the short walk back she completely forgot about the two men's exchange.

TWENTY-FIVE

Twenty-four hours of quiet had passed, Cal found himself wishing something would happen. There had been some news. Rebecca Swain had given up the source of Brad's fake identification, a two-bedroom apartment located above a thrift store in the city of Seattle. Why he'd decided a variation of his real name instead of a less obvious alias was a mystery, the answer Brad took to the grave.

Rebecca's cooperation earner her a twenty year sentence to be served at penal colony number 314 located in the Arizona desert where prisoners performed numerous tasks in an air-conditioned facility. It was soft time compared to the majority of penal colonies. Cal had been correct, Rebecca's father had pulled some strings, he'd even sent her a care package containing toiletries, clean underwear, pajamas, a bath robe and a variety of junk food.

Dr. Lorre had decided to keep Rebecca on pain meds so she'd stay docile, he hooked her up to an IV drip, which transformed her into a very sweet young lady. A television set to a movie channel was wheeled into her room, Rebecca spent her remaining time in the Line watching old Meg Ryan flicks, stuffing her face and riding a buzz.

Before the narcotics completely kicked in Rebecca had asked if her things had been removed from her apartment? Yes, they had. Were Brad's love poems amongst them? Yes, they were. Could she take them with her to the penal colony? Yes, she could.Unfucking-believable thought Cal.

*

Cal arrived home at his shift's end, he found Valentine in her dressing room modeling an outfit in front of her full-length mirror.

"Lila wants to bring back maids."

Cal knew certain fetishes had an eternal life. Still, Valentine had forgone the cliché French version for one of her own design. The top and bottom were made of black vinyl and trimmed with a white, lacy material and she wore black patent leather shoes with four straps that buckled o the side along with white knee-high stockings. She accessorized with long, white gloves, maid's cap and a black choker. Naturally, it was difficult to imagine a woman actually cleaning in such an outfit.

As a result of Stray Katz's theme policy Valentine had amassed a large collection of costumes. Some she'd sewn herself, but the majority of them were made by Kasume Kurotaki, a thirty-four year old immigrant from Japan. She was a seamstress of incredible talent who ran her tailoring business, called Just Teasing, from her home and had clients from every club.

"Guess what Lila's latest idea is?"

"What."

"It's a small world."

TWENTY-SIX

As late afternoon turned to early evening Valentine could tell Cal was getting anxious and it was threatening to become contagious. They both needed to get out've the house, if only for a few hours. So she suggested the dine out at Napalm Palace, a small Thai restaurant just a short walk from their house. While she got changed Valentine had Cal call and make a reservation. Minutes later she emerged wearing a lilac colored summer dress and a pair of open-toed sandals.

Their house sat on the corner of Chalmers and Peters, they took a left on Peter and began to walk the six blocks to the restaurant. The climate outside was pleasant as usual. While it never rained in the Line certain days were appointed for the release of water vapor for the benefit of the local vegetation. But it wasn't the same as having real weather. Valentine had always gotten a thrill from watching thunderstorms, she also missed the change of seasons, but was in the minority of a population who were grateful to be spared the chore of shoveling snow or the inconvenience of being caught in a sudden downpour.

All around them the shield shimmered a powder blue that reminded Valentine of the old Disney cartoons she'd watched as a child. Cal held her hand, they barely spoke as they passed Ford, Packard, and Studebaker, streets named after the men who'd built the auto industry. A block to the right was Van Dyke, the main drag, as they turned onto Hupp it came into view.

It was when night fell that the strip really came to life. Every club was ablaze in a neon inferno, each offering escape into a fantasy world, a pool of pleasure inside the bubble where the outside became more of a memory the longer you stayed within its borders. Nearly two centuries ago Centerline's first church, St. Clements had been constructed a half mile east of Sherwood Avenue. Back then growth had been something few pursued, less cared about. It'd been a community of farmers who'd been content to remain mostly isolated, the only access in or out had been horse and buggy.

The original church had long gone the way of the street car trucks while Centerline had returned to its state of isolation and pleasant routine. News from the outside filtered in, but was seldom commented on. The announcement of North Koreas erasure from the world map was met with a casual indifference, it could have been a fictional land like Oz. Insular threats took precedence, but more and more the Weather Underground was becoming the annoying party guest that refused to get the hints to leave.

The Napalm Palace was a misleading moniker. In actuality it was a small, subdued building paneled in wood painted a deep burgundy with black trim, it resembled a cottage rather than a restaurant. In the tradition of Asian eateries it was window-less sparing diners the garishness that surrounded them. The Napalm also had the distinction of being one of the few businesses that survived Centerline's transformation, the other two being All-Star Books and the Honey Bee donut shop.

Inside half of the ten tables were occupied, the Napalm offered take-out service, which most people seemed to prefer. Not Valentine and Cal, they were regulars and were greeted by Mrs. Mitimada who, along with her husband, owned the restaurant. She also acted the role of hostess, always wearing a benevolent smile. She wore an orange sari over a white blouse, her black hair conservatively pulled back, a contrast to the chunky gold jewelry, all of it real, that hung from her ears, neck and wrists.

After they were seated Mrs. Mitimada signaled to a waiter, who was also one of her nephews, to bring Cal and Valentine each a bottle of Singhar beer, a Thai brand that could only be had at her establishment. How she'd acquired the import license was one of the great mysteries of the Line. While they waited for the drinks to arrive she engaged Cal and Valentine in some friendly small talk, Mrs. Mitimada took care not to mention the Weather Underground, which she considered distasteful. She treated her restaurant as a cocoon within a bubble, the troubles of the outside had no place there.

When the chilled bottles of beer arrived she politely excused herself and returned to the front of the room while the waiter took their order. They chose pad roum mitt, siam chicken and fried rice. While they ate neither Cal or Valentine spoke of the enemy hiding in their midst. It was only after their third round of Singhar arrived that Valentine felt relaxed enough to brooch the topic that had been on her mind.

"Cal, have you thought about what we'll do when our contracts are up?"

"That's still a ways off. Has this place started getting to you?"

"No, but it's not too early to start looking at our options. Who knows , the war could end, then it might be safe to travel over-seas again."

"Maybe, if there's any place left worth visiting. Besides, I thought all your road time with the U.S.O. soured my desire to travel."

"That was work, I've never had a chance to be an actual tourist."

"Well, just as long as we don't go anywhere near the middle east, the entire region's probably been turned into a parking lot by now. What I'd like to do is buy an island and really get away from it all."

"We could build ourselves a shack, live off the land. It'd be just like this movie I watched once on TV. What the hell was it called?"
Valentine found herself stumped, she tried to recall the film's name, but drew nothing but a blank.

"I can remember it was during a tour, a stop-over in Wisconsin. We stayed at the Silver Lake motor lodge, the place was so old the beds still had magic fingers, but they didn't work."
"Can you remember who starred in it?"

"Yeah, what's her name, Brooke Shields, she was really young."

"Sorry, doesn't sound familiar."

"Shit, this is going to torture me all night. Maybe Mrs. Miti-mada knows."

"I doubt it, remember once she told us she hasn't seen a movie since 'The Sound of Music.'"

The subject eventually faded away. They enjoyed a final round of drinks before paying the check and heading back home. They walked arm in arm, the strong beer made the world fuzzy around the edges. The only person they saw was a fifty-ish woman sitting on her porch nursing a can of beer and smoking a cigarette. Somewhere a dog barked

71

After making love they both fell asleep. Valentine dreamt she was standing on a beach of white sand, looking out at water that was pale green and becoming dark blue farther out.

She began to examine her body. Her skin was tanned a deep bronze and she was wearing a two-piece garment of white cotton that looked hand-made. Valentine had just realized that her hair was longer, having grown passed her shoulders, when noises from behind drew her attention inland.

She saw a group of DPW workers, they seemed to be idly milling about. There was one exception, one man had climbed a palm tree and was using a machete to hack off coconuts. They fell into a pile on the ground.

One of the men called out to the others to join him around a radio. As the men huddled close together Valentine strained to hear what they were listening to, she had a feeling it was serious because the men started to look panicked. She began to walk towards them, but before she could get close enough to ask them anything they hastily gathered their things and ran into the forest.

Valentine awoke with such a start that her upper body bolted upright in bed.

"The Blue Lagoon!" she exclaimed. But Valentine was unable to hear herself. Something was screaming so loud it drowned her out. The bedside clock read 12:05 a.m.

TWENTY-SEVEN

It was the sound every badge hoped he'd never hear, the brain-splitting scream of the main checkpoint warning siren. After Rebecca Swain had been wrung like a sponge she, along with the handful of Weather Underground members who'd survived the Engelmann firefight, had been processed and were to be taken to the temporary holding facility in old warren. Prisoners were transported through a mile long underground tunnel, which began at the sub-level garage beneath the Walther Reuther freeway. The main checkpoint was guarded by robotic sentries armed with 60 caliber machine guns. Upon arrival at the border a person was given a series of voice commands ending with an order to await the arrival of border security personnel. Failure to comply proved fatal. The sentries were maintained by the DPW, this had never sat well with the police who felt it didn't make sense and thought public works put too much faith in the automated system. It was an open secret amongst cops that there were multiple ways to disable the sentries. While they wouldn't stay down for long, only a few minutes at most, but it would be enough.

It didn't help that the DPW had been working double shifts, spreading themselves thin as the searched for more possible entry points in the sewer system. Cal knew Ryan would be arriving any minute so he quickly got dressed in the spare set of body armor he kept at home. He'd paid for it out've his own pocket and many of his fellow badges told him it'd been a waste of money, but he was glad he'd done it.

As he said goodbye to Valentine there was no mistaking the look on her face, she was scared. Cal reassured her as best as he could while trying to convince himself that all would turn out all right.

Ryan had the chorus burning as he lead-footed towards the cathedral, profanities pouring from his mouth. Half a block from headquarters they reached the perimeter fence, a series of chest-high concrete barriers that automatically rose from the sidewalk. Ryan pulled their cruiser over to the side of the road, as they exited they were greeted by a rookie named Demiti-rie who proceeded to fill them in while they did a weapons check.

"The convoy was intercepted about two-thirds in, they used RPGs to take out every vehicle, including the prisoner carrier.

"Do we have any intel as to how many hostels we're dealing with? He asked.

"The reports are conflicting, two dozen, possibly more. Good news is all the upper levels are locked down so they can only come out or go back."

Cal locked eyes with Ryan. "Only one thing for us to do, we have to go in and force them back into the tunnel."

Ryan nodded. "Let's put these fucks through some changes."

Before they headed into the cathedral Cal took a moment to silently send Valentine his love.

TWENTY-EIGHT

Like everyone in the Line Valentine couldn't ignore the warning siren, it threatened to crack her sanity. She shoved her ipod's ear buds in and hit the shuffle button. As 'Wildfire' began to play she felt increasingly helpless. It was an emotion that was alien to her. When Cal rushed out the door he'd told her he loved her and Valentine realized she may never see him alive again. All that time spent overseas just to get killed at home.

Time crawled, she hoped the music would keep her distracted, but the enormity of the situation prevented it so she turned it off. At some point the siren ceased only to be replaced by the sound of random gunfire. Daylight was still hours away, something about the darkness accentuated the threat, it conjured an adolescent fear of monsters in the closet.

Valentine had never been a political person, she believed it was up to the individual to make their own way, occasionally some luck might fall into your lap, but you couldn't count on it. While on the U.S.O. tours there'd always been a few anti-war protestors, old hippies and college kids who held up signs, chanted and drummed on plastic bucket. Valentine never understood what they thought they were accomplishing. The one thing they shared with the likes of Rebecca Swain was their childlike irrationality. Their infiltration of the Line was akin to kicking a hornet's nest. The Weather Underground not only seem to realize this, what made it more horrific was that they didn't seem to care.

When Valentine heard the sound of glass shattering she instinctively ducked behind the couch. It was followed by a loud rushing noise, she knew what it was even before she peered over her shoulder and saw the licks of flame.

Someone had tossed a molitov cocktail through the window. No doubt whoever threw it was trying to flush her out and she assumed someone was positioned at the back door, perhaps another one of Rebecca's suitors. Valentine knew the window for escape was shrinking by the second. The basement was out of the question, her only option was to go up. She crawled on her hands and knees to the bedroom so she could retrieve the shotgun. Fortunately, the police hadn't seen the need for the usual twenty-four hour confiscation. Valentine slung it over her shoulder then made her way to the stairs.

The home's upper level wasn't much more than an attic space that she and Cal used for storage. It was windowless so Valentine scanned the length of the ceiling before picking a spot on the right side. She racked the shotgun and pumped all six rounds into the roof while taking the precaution to avert her face from the shower of debris that rained down. As she felt the shards of wood fragments against her skin, Valentine hoped the noise hadn't alerted her attackers to what she was attempting.

She set the gun down then used one of Cal's old foot lockers to give her enough elevation to boost herself up. As Valentine pulled herself through the opening the jagged edges of splintered beams scraped against her sides, she gritted her teeth and kept going until she made it onto the roof.

There was thick, charcoal grey smoke coming from the front of the house, it provided Valentine some cover as she took a running jump onto the roof of the next door neighbors. After landing on her feet she rolled over onto her stomach and cautiously looked down. What Valentine saw took her a couple of seconds to process. It seemed as if the entire block was surrounded on her front lawn, many of them toting guns. Bob Coates, the man who's roof Valentine was perched on, was spraying water from a garden hose onto the flames while a cigarette dangled from his mouth.

Meanwhile two other men had their rifles trained on a pair of individuals lying face down on the lawn. In the distance Valentine could hear the siren of a fast approaching fire engine, it was joined by the sound of her laughter. As she sat up and dangled her legs off the edge of his roof Bob looked up and waved at her.

TWENTY-NINE

The Weather Underground began rushing out of the cathedral just as Cal and the other officers were beginning their advance, they fell back into a defensive position behind the perimeter fence. Fueled by what seemed like blind determination the invaders propelled themselves into the police's gunfire, it reminded Cal of the Japanese banzai charges. There were a few who seemed to have grasped the rashness of this and realizing they had nothing in the way of cover ran back into the building.

"Helter Selter you pukes!" yelled Ryan as he took aim at a Che lookalike toting a grenade launcher.

He tagged the man between the eyes knocking him backwards, but his death reflex was strong enough for the RPG to be launched, the missile shot up into the air, arched left and finally came down in an empty parking lot. The explosion sent up a shower of concrete chunks and dirt.

Cal flashed back to Libya, to twelve year old girls with explosives strapped their bodies charging towards him while they screamed incoherently. He'd pegged his fair share, they came to be called 'Cherry Poppers' because of the way they seemed to disintegrate when their bombs went off.

The announcement of arriving reinforcements at tunnel's other side came over their headsets, the WU that had retreated back into the cathedral had trapped themselves on the ground floor. Trucks with roof-mounted tear gas cans began to flood that section of the building. Cal and their other officers donned their gas masks, checked their ammo and restarted the advance to reclaim the cathedral.

THIRTY

For the third time in the span of a week Valentine found herself giving a statement to a police officer, this time to a fresh faced rookie who didn't look old enough to shave. He seemed to want her to assure him that he was doing a good job, before he left he informed her that control of police headquarters had been secured. Within a few minutes he was also able to find out Cal's whereabouts and assure her he was all right. After Valentine thanked him she noticed a slightly giddy ship to his step.

Once the medics had dressed her wounds she sat down on the curb. Valentine felt exhausted, but heartened that the fire had been extinguished before it'd gotten the chance to get out of control. Several of her neighbors had come forward to offer her and Cal shelter, she thanked them and politely declined. Valentine wanted to sip champagne while soaking in a tub of hot water scented with oil.

As DPW workers placed a sheet of plywood over her home's shattered picture window she got permission to briefly enter the house so she could pack a bag for herself and another for Cal. She managed to retrieve her cell phone, first she called Cal, the line was busy so she left him a message. Next, she phoned the Majestic Hotel and made a reservation before finally calling a cab company. Her message to Cal didn't mention the bombing, Valentine decided it could wait until they were face to face.

THIRTY-ONE

"Today is a great day for America," sang out the voice of Director Coulter. On the video monitor her face was aglow like a woman in love.

"The Weather Underground's offensive has been successfully repelled, in addition word has just been received that their maiden head Bernardine Dohrn was amongst the casualties of a drone strike carried out on the orders of the President. The location of the pacific-northwest compound was discovered through the diligent work of the intelligence arm of the anti-sedition forces. We have struck a mighty blow against the enemy, our great nation still stands tall, her resolve remains strong. May god bless you and god bless the United States of America."

*

Later after Captain Tyson informed Cal of the attack on his home, and that Valentine was unharmed, he got out his cell and listened to her voice mail. Hearing her Cal felt a wave of emotions. He hung up the phone and struggled to find an explanation for the series of recent events that had plagued their lives. 'Stray Katz' had been the only club hit, it hadn't been a WU sanctioned attack, Valentine's working there had been a coincidence, but she'd shot Rebecca Swain, which led to her lover to seek revenge. But how Brad Steiner had learned where Valentine lived was still a mystery. 'Stray Katz' computer files had been examined for signs of hacking, none were found.

Events had moved fast, aside from his brief questioning of the Swain girl Cal had acted more as a soldier than an investigator, but that was what in reality what he was, a grunt. Dr. Lorre would interrogate the few Weather Underground members who'd surrendered, but what, if any, useful information they had to offer was not yet known.

Cal and Ryan walked to their cruiser till parked across the street from the cathedral. After storing their gear in the trunk they both lit a cigarette and surveyed the damage.

"Bunch of suicidal punks" spat Ryan. "They'll be turned into cat food and finally have made themselves useful."

He turned to Cal, "You know what the best part of the job is?" he asked.

"What?"

"No paper work, the computers take care of all that shit. You can always tell who was already a cop before the war, they know how to type."

Cal knew Ryan was attempting to deflate the situation. He felt the tug of yearning for something that was so far away. Life had turned into an ugly farce and Cal couldn't give up his front row seat.

THIRTY-TWO

The Majestic Hotel was a six-story oasis of luxury, a place to go when you lived in a city that you couldn't leave. It was subsidized by the government, so it didn't matter whether the guests numbered two or two hundred. While Valentine signed in her luggage was taken to her room. She'd requested one on the top floor, which had the largest suites.

Before she began approaching she called Lila Dean to request a leave of absence. Valentine informed her of the second attempt on her life, suggesting it'd be a good idea for her to stay away from the club until normalcy had fully returned. Lila was understanding and assured Valentine her job would be waiting for her.

Valentine felt as if life were piling on. It just wasn't the loss of income, the novelty of having excess idle time had already begun to wear off. Cal would no doubt devote himself to finding the remaining Weather Underground members, meanwhile, she'd be stuck within the walls of the hotel trying to come up with something to do besides getting stoned in front of the TV.

She'd just finished putting her things way when she heard the sound of a card key unlocking the door. Cal entered and Valentine rushed into his arms. He lifted her off the ground while she wrapped her legs around his waist. Within seconds they stripped and engaged in an anxious bout of sex. Afterward Valentine felt her weariness return. Cal pressed his body close to hers reminding her of their time in the wilderness when they spent as many nights in a shared sleeping bag.

But Valentine's pleasant recollection was shadowed by the faces of the men who'd tried to rape her. That boy, his tears

82

streaming down his dirty face, the way the bullet to his head instantly shut off his sobs. Valentine didn't regret killing any of them, nor did she ever blame Cal for leaving her alone. Yet there were times when she caught him looking at her and it seemed as if he hadn't yet forgiven himself.

THIRTY-THREE

After Valentine had fallen asleep Cal sat up watching her. He then slid out've bed and entered the bathroom. He turned on the shower, waiting until the water was sufficiently hot before getting in. He finished washing, when he stepped into a thick fog he wrapped himself in a bathrobe, took a beer out of the mini-bar and took a seat by the room's window. Outside the plasma shield was a rich purple.

Cal sipped the beer while he listened to the sound of Valentine's breathing. His longing for her had begun as an adolescent crush. He remembered when she'd gotten her ears pierced as a gift for her twelfth birthday and in Cal's boyhood eyes it lent her an air of sophistication. Their relationship had deepened over the years, but remained platonic and his desires remained unconsummated.

While he was in the army Cal had kept his friendship with Valentine a secret from the other men in his unit. Her pin-ups had decorated his barracks as well as others, life-sized posters hung in some officers clubs. Valentine's star had been ascending and she'd been poised to go even higher. So, when he asked her to join him in the Line he hadn't actually expected her to accept.

But almost immediately he'd regretted it. Cal had greatly underestimated the amount of time they'd have to spend getting through the wilderness. Their journey had been accompanied by a cloud of fear that had always threatened to overtake them. Still, Valentine never complained, nor did she blame him for their many hardships.

Now, by a set of circumstances cal could have never foreseen, she'd been marked for death. Valentine had recently hinted at the future, a life outside the Line. They both had time on their contracts. Cal had spent the last four years as a grunt, first in the army, then the police force, and nothing more by way of education other than a high school diploma. It was beginning to make his head swim. Cal felt himself starting to nod off. He finished off the beer, as he slid into bed Valentine let out a sigh and snuggled against him. Within minutes Cal fell asleep.

THIRTY-FOUR

POSTED ON BMYVALENTINE.COM ON 7-19-13
BY DEAN LIRIUM
MORE DAMSEL DARING DO!

It seems that all the Weather Underground's yapping about fascist Amerikkka has taken, ahem, a left turn. Seems the greatest threat to creation of a socialist utopia isn't the American military complex, but our very own fav girl.

First, they have a bullet party at 'Stray Katz.' Second, her domicile is deified by a kommie weasel who tried to make her ah angel. Now, comes word someone tried to torch said home sweet home while our sweetie was in it. The bums have no shame.

But it seems fair Valentine is a cat with nine lives, she escaped the deadly blaze with barely a scratch to her lovely frame, three cheers for our all-American girl!

Meanwhile 'Stray Katz' has been reopened, but sadly our fav girl has been forced to sit it out at least until the Weather Underground dipshits have all been rounded up and flushed.
But take heart, your boy Deano has compiled a collection of Valentine's greatest hits. Just dig her in that maid outfit, whose house needs cleaning?

THIRTY-FIVE

It was sometime in the afternoon when Valentine awoke, outside the plasma shield glistened salmon pink. Despite some residual soreness she felt fine, the previous day seemed more like some bizarre dream, but when she looked down and saw the scratches running along her hips she was reminded it wasn't. Cal was still asleep, Valentine decided to hold off waking him. She gave him a feather light kiss on the forehead before sliding out of bed and proceeded through a series of stretching exercises. They worked out the kinks in her body and stoked her appetite.

Valentine picked up the room phone and called room service. The Majestic offered breakfast twenty-four hours so she ordered blueberry pancakes, scrambled eggs, sausage, a pitcher of orange juice and a pot of coffee. It would be ten minutes before the food would arrive. Just enough time for her to take a quick shower. She'd just begun to towel off her hair when there was a knock at the door. She heard Cal's voice as he let the waiter in and waited until the man left before she exited the bathroom.

Cal ate very little, he seemed content to nibble at a plate of eggs while he watched Valentine as she stuffed her face. She'd been hungrier than she realized leaving nothing but a few scraps. As they stacked the dishes onto the room service cart Cal received a call on his cell from Dr. Lorre. They spoke briefly, after their conversation he contacted Ryan ad asked to be picked up.

*

After Cal had left Valentine took out her stash and rolled herself a joint. She smoked it while staring idly out the window. The Majestic was the second tallest building in the city, I gave her a panoramic view of the Line. The shield's color had changed to mandarin orange. Valentine resolved herself to the circumstances she now found herself in, and to her life as it was. She'd be turning twenty-two in a couple of months, she figured that at best she had three years left as a dancer, and figured that if she couldn't predict the future she could at least try and maintain some control over the present. She'd eventually go back to work at 'Stray Katz,' sock away as much money as she could an wait to see how the world turned out.

Valentine yearned to return to her job, if for no other reason than it wouldn've kept her occupied. She was already starting to feel cooped up, Cal had asked her to stay within the confines of the hotel. She held to his request, but needed something to do. The ground floor offered plenty of diversions. Valentine snuffed out the joint, got dressed, slipped her key card into the back pocket of her jeans and a few seconds later she was in an elevator heading down.

THIRTY-SIX

From the moment he and Ryan arrived at the cathedral Cal could feel the optimistic vibe flowing through the building that had replaced the apprehension of the previous few days. It seemed that what had been expected to be a well-trained guerilla army instead turned out to be a gang who couldn't shoot straight.

Bernardin Dohrn's death had the predicted demoralizing effect, intel revealed internal power struggles had erupted within the hierarchy of the Weather Underground leadership ranks and looked as if it was in the process of consuming itself from within. The few strays still left inside the line had surrendered. They projected resentment, the feeling they'd been fed to the lions. The ones who thought they had information were spilling in the hopes of being sent to a penal colony.

Cal rode the elevator to the fourth floor where Dr. Lorre was waiting for him in his office. The room's interior was Spartan, it contained a desk, two chairs, and a half dozen filing cabinets, the doctor still insisted keeping hard copies of his files. Hung on the right side wall were three picture frames, one held Lorre's medical license certification. The other two were larger, both were fifteen by twenty-seven photos, one of the old Stroh's Brewery, the other the former Vernors bottling plant.

Slumped in one of the chairs was a young man in his early twenties. His long, dirty blonde hair was pulled back into a pony tail, his face was covered with equal parts beard stubble and acne. When he and Cal's eyes met Cal saw they were red and puffy.

"This young man's name is Ethan, he was captured by your neighbors before being turned over to us. He has, with my generous assistance, rediscovered his soul. In the course of our many conversation he's revealed the name of a male comrade whose been harboring an intense interest in Miss Usher."

Cal approached Ethan and stood over him.

"Give me a name," Cal demanded.

Ethan's eyes began to water. He wiped his nose on his arm then looked down at his feet.

"Beaupre Miller," he whispered.

THIRTY-SEVEN

In a way Valentine felt like a kid playing hookey as she walked past the gym, pool and spa. Like Cal she didn't gamble so the casino wasn't an option. She didn't need to buy anything, so she avoided the shops. Instead, she walked into the video arcade.

Valentine hadn't been inside such a place since high school, even then they hadn't held much allure. But being on road tour after road tour she soon discovered life on a bus was an almost constant battle against boredom. Every U.S.O. vehicle had been outfitted with a few gaming consoles and TVs, eventually even the most stubborn dancer picked up a controller and found a game they liked. Valentine's preference was for first person shooters.

The arcade's interior was a throwback, dimly lit with most of the illumination coming from the glow of the machines. Valentine bought twenty dollars worth of tokens from an automated dispenser then wandered the aisles looking for something that would pique her interest. There was one row devoted to vintage games like Pac-Man, and Asteroids, another to pinball machines, there was even and air hockey table. Finally she found something called 'Zombie Apocalypse' and she spent the next two hours making her way through a desolate city scape and dispatching the undead,

After she left the arcade Valentine wasn't sure what to do next, only that she didn't want to go back to her room. She looked across the hall at a pair of glass sliding doors that let out to an atrium. They opened silently as Valentine stepped onto a stone path that weaved through the manicured greenery.

At the center of the courtyard was a white marble fountain, its jets of water performed a delicate ballet for an audience of one. Its centerpiece was a bronze statue of the goddess Diana. She'd been sculpted standing erect, her bow drawn, an arrow aimed but never to be fired. How odd, Valentine thought. Figures from greek myth showed up in the strangest of places. But Diana was a warrior, Centerline was an armament city, so her pressure made sense. Still it was a shame she was hidden away.

Valentine's eyes caught the glint the many coins that'd been tossed into the pool. Dozens of silver and copper circles rested on the fountains bottom. Valentine dug into her jeans pocket and came up with forty-three cents. She selected the lone quarter, closed her eyes while she silently made her wish then flicked the coin. It landed into the water with a quiet plop.

Valentine knew there were several restaurants on the other side of the garden, but she wasn't hungry, instead she felt a craving for a drink. Yet another pitfall of a self-imposed reprieve from working: the desire to booze before five. She exited the garden and strolled along the row of eateries. Everything was represented, from steakhouse to Chinese, but she settled on Lou's, from the outside it looked like an Irish bar. When she walked through the door she found a place that was small, dark and unpretentious. She liked it immediately.

'Lou's' was actually a replica of a pre-war Centerline bar that had been built in the 1940s. It was owned by the same family who kept it as a time capsule. All along the walls were framed photographs. Some showed men in military uniforms going back to the Second World War. Others were of Christmas parties with twinkling lights and plastic Santas. Then there were the portraits of infants who were now retirement age.

Valentine saddled up to the bar, which she instantly could tell was made of real wood and not some modern composite. She ordered a gin and tonic, after her drink was delivered Valentine looked about and noticed that aside from herself and the bartender there were only two other patrons, a middle-aged factory worker and a younger man in a DPW uniform. Both seemed content to drink in silence. Valentine had almost finished her cocktail when she felt eyes on her.

THIRTY-EIGHT

A search of Beaupre Miller's apartment failed to reveal anything about the man. The single room dwelling contained no photos, papers or any personal artifacts of any kind. A few pieces of clothing hanging in a closet, a bed, and a television were the only bits of evidence to show that anyone had ever occupied the room. A search using the cathedral's computer's revealed no one of that designation living in the Line.

Cal interviewed the few people who shared residence in the building. Those who'd managed to catch a glimpse of their neighbor failed to provide a consistent portrait, he'd clearly taken steps to conceal his identity.

Ethan, the boy who'd coughed up the name hadn't much more to tell except that Miller had offered five thousand in cash along with the promise of a clean escape out've the Line to finish what Brad Striger had started. But it was clear that Ethan and his accomplice weren't assassins, just two people so desperate that the accepted the first opportunity given to them. Like the apartment's occupants Ethan could only give a vague description. He'd seen Miller at a few cell meetings, but he was a quiet type who floated around the edges, but failed to make much of an impression. All Cal was left with was a living enigma.

After he exited the building he called Valentine, she was at one of the hotel bars having a drink. Cal filled her in on what little he knew. Next he phoned 'Stray Katz' and spoke to Lila Dean, he gave her his best possible description of Miller and asked her to keep an eye open for anyone who asked about Valentine's whereabouts.

Beaupre Miller, real name unknown. A man who'd rubbed

elbows with terrorists had been successful in hiding in plain sight. He wanted Valentine dead and Cal was no closer to discovering why.

THIRTY-NINE

After getting off the phone with Cal, Valentine got up and went to the ladies room. When she returned she notice the young DPW worker had moved and seated himself two stools from her. When their eyes briefly met he immediately went red-faced and tilted his head down so all that showed was a mop of chestnut hair.

Valentine wondered if he could be one of 'Stray Katz' regulars. She'd been recognized outside the club before, on those occasions the men acted shy. Some of her co-workers encouraged that kind of adulation, they were often rewarded with gifts of clothing, jewelry and cash. Even though it was a somewhat accepted practice Valentine never participated, these fans sometimes mistook the dancer's reciprocation as an introduction to a more intimate relationship. That said, Valentine wasn't opposed to giving an autograph, she'd done it before. But if that was what he was after it was up to him to get off his duff and ask for it.

Then, as if on cue, he slid off his seat, picked up his beer and sat down beside her. Valentine really wasn't in the mood for conversation, she hoped he'd keep it brief. His apprehension was palpable, she attempted to place his face, but found nothing recognizable. After a couple of minutes of just staring at his beer he turned his head toward her.

"You're Valentine Usher, you dance at 'Stray Katz."

Her ears pricked up, it'd come out sounding rehearsed. She found a smile as she met his gaze. He had an immature face, but there was a hardness in the eyes. Valentine glanced down at the DPW I.D. clipped to the breast pocket of his coveralls, it said his name was Pascal Birken.

"Yes, I am."

"They reopened today."
"I know."

"Did you quit?"

"No, I'm taking some time off."

"That's understandable, what with all that's been going on lately."

Valentine was getting a vibe from this guy and she didn't like it, she regretted not having her piece. She was about to excuse herself.

"What's it like to kill someone?"

It was the last thing she'd expected. Pascal smiled, glad he caught her off guard.

"Quite an accomplishment striking a woman like you speechless."

His follow up remark irritated her, he'd deflated the element of surprise.

"A woman like me, you mean a stripper?"

"Oh now, I don't have any objections to your profession."

"So glad to hear it."

"But, apparently, Rebecca could never be convinced."

97

Valentine realized her first assumption was correct, he'd rehearsed this encounter, probably while standing in front of a mirror.

"You a friend of Becky and late Brad?" she asked as she motioned to the bartender for a fresh drink.

"I didn't much care for Rebecca, she was inconsistent. She'd sleep with just about anyone, male or female, said it was the comradely thing to do. So, I thought it was strange she'd have such a problem getting naked in public."

"Maybe it was because money was involved."

"Probably. Brad I felt sorry for."

"Too much devoted puppy, not enough true believer."

He nodded. "Rebecca really wasn't much more than a sloganeering malcontent, like most of them."

"You don't like them, do you?"

"No, I don't," he stated flatly.

Valentine took a generous swallow of gin and tonic then focused back on the man beside her.

"All right, Pascal, I'm beginning to have fun with this little game so let's keep on playing. Now, going back to your original question; you want to know what it's like to turn out someone's lights, specifically Brad's. Well, he did break into my home, it was a clear case of him or me.

Pascal let out a sigh then took a sip of beer, swallowed. "It just proves that if you want something done right you have to do it yourself."

His statement confirmed what Valentine had suspected, that he was behind the hit on her. She gave him a once over, he didn't appear to be packing a weapon, nor was he physically imposing. Valentine wasn't about to start composing her will just yet.

Pascal finished off the bottle. Suddenly, his eyes got a faraway cast.

"This is all Calum and Joe's fault. Jalin only went along because he was afraid."

Valentine experienced an instant memory download. The wilderness, three men, one blubbering like a baby, all three on the ground with holes in between their eyes.

Valentine knocked back the rest of her cocktail. "You seemed to have recognized those two dirt bags for what they were, so why did you join up with them?"

Her question eased a minor tremor of anger to ripple across his face. She meant to poke a nerve.

Pascal resumed a calm demeanor. "It was simply a matter of safety in numbers. You were out there, you know how bad it could get, after a while bodies on the side of the road became so common you learned to ignore them. Jalin and I already had our clearance to enter Centerline, Calum and Josh didn't. Our plan was to ditch them at the first opportunity that presented itself. We were supposed to be searching for supplies, I must have gotten distracted because I turned around and they were gone."

"Did they rape any other women?"

"I don't know, but I wouldn't have put it passed them."

"Still, you chose to let your brother go off with them."

Valentine saw that tremor of anger bubble back.

"I told you we were supposed to be looking for food. I wasn't even aware that there was anyone else nearby, not until I heard the gunshots. By the time I got to the scene you and your boy-friend were getting in your car. When I finally made it here I attempted to put everything that'd happened in the wilderness behind me, to just forget it. I got assigned to the DPW and quickly got lost in the routine. Six months passed, then one day I'm walking home, I was passing 'Stray Katz' when I looked up and was confronted by your picture. That's when everything came flooding back."

Pascal emitted a bitter chuckle, Valentine decided to prod him further.

"How'd the Weather Underground get involved?"

"One night while looking for a place to sleep I entered what I thought was an empty building and stumbled upon a group of people squatting, Rebecca and Brad were amongst them. They quickly realized I was harmless and offered me something to eat, later we got to know each other better. I realized what they were so I knew how to act and what to say. I left in the morning while they were still asleep. Imagine my surprise when months later I bumped into Rebecca in a grocery store right here in the Line. She greeted me like an old friend and invited me to a meeting. I was curious, so I went, didn't take long to realize they were suffering delusions of grandeur."

"Whose idea was it to shoot up 'Stray Katz?'"

"Some dyke named Franzisha, she wanted to hit a club, I suggested yours and hoped they'd get lucky. I wasn't surprised when they screwed up."

Valentine lit a joint, she exhaled a plume of smoke into the air. "It was your job at the DPW that you found out I tagged Rebecca, it's no secret that public works and the police are one big sewing circle. So you used Brad's affections for Rebecca to manipulate him into a hit on me?"

Pascal nodded and smiled. "It didn't take a genius, I simply played on his feelings. Brad wasn't a bad person, just very confused. He saw himself as a Galahad, but Rebecca was no Guinevere."

"What about the yahoos who set my house on fire?"

"That part was their idea. To be honest I'd lost most of my faith in my own revenge plot. I simply offered money with a false promise of escape. The few stragglers were very desperate, so of course, I had takers."

Valentine asked the bartender for a glass of ice water. As she drank Valentine knew Pascal posed no danger, he was a coward and like all cowards he couldn't do his own dirty work. It was amazing he'd lasted in the wilderness as long as he had. While she finished off the glass he'd remained quiet, but resumed speaking the moment she set it down.

"The people I hired were, of course, captured, they've no doubt talked in hopes of being sent to a penal colony. Your boyfriend's a cop, so prison isn't in the cards for me."

They looked into each other's eyes, Valentine could see he'd resigned himself to his fate. She slid off her seat and stretched. "You're correct, shacking up with a badge does have many advantages."

Pascal's face became downcast. "Enjoy it while you can. I can't see over the horizon, yet I can't help but think the lucky ones are already dead."

Valentine shrugged, then flashed a smile. "Who knows, I stopped worrying about the outside world a long time ago. But you know what, I'm going to do you a favor."

Pascal's expression turned confused, his eyes narrowed.

"Just what would that be?" he asked.

Valentine offered him another smile, she then grabbed the sides of his head and with a single, swift motion she jerked it to the left. A sharp cracking sound announced that she'd broken Pascal's neck like a dry twig.

"To do you like I did your brother," she said before releasing him. His body hit the floor with a decisive thud, his eyes staring at nothing.

FORTY

Valentine's call came while Cal and Ryan had been staking out 'Stray Katz.' They'd changed into civies after finding out Miller's real name from a Weather Underground snitch. Once it was discovered he worked for the DPW everything else fell into place and they'd set up a signal with Lila Dean in case Beaupre a.k.a. Pascal showed his face.

'Stray Katz' theme for the day was classic Hollywood, on stage Greta Garbo and Marlene Dietrich had been halfway out of their tuxes when Valentine phoned Cal, her voice had been completely calm.

"See you soon babe, love ya," she said before hanging up.
As Cal was leaving the club he couldn't help think what a great Joan Crawford she would've made. Sweet Valentine, mad, bad, and dangerous to know.

FORTY-ONE

POSTED ON BMYVALENTINE.COM ON 7-24-15
BY DEAN LIRIOUS
VALENTINE'S TRIUMPHANT RETURN

'Ol Deano has been popping champagne corks along with the rest of the Valentine Usher fan family over the happy news of our fav girl's return to 'Stray Katz.' On Super Hero day no less, it don't get much more all-American than that.

My sources have filled me in to the facts behind our Miss Usher's recent troubles. Seems it's the result of a personal beef that goes back to some bad business during her time in the big, bad wilderness.

Now, with Bernardin Dohrn down for the dirt nap and the Weather Underground out of the picture it seems Uncle Sam has come calling. Ou fav girl is being wooed to once again don the stars and stripes and strut her stuff. I've also heard world famous pin-up artist Olivia wants to produce a Valentine-themed calendar. So keep your fingers crossed 'cause our all-American girl might be coming to your town.

FORTY-TWO

It was weeks after Valentine had sent Beaupre Miller to meet his maker that life in the Line finally returned to normal. She'd returned full-time to 'Stray Katz,' the donations to the Valentine Usher retirement fund came pouring in, she was treated like a returning war hero.

The munitions plants still operated around the clock, they'd never stopped, the Weather Underground had never been a threat. The lingering question, never completely answered, was what they'd hoped to accomplish by breaking into the Line. Like similar groups that'd preceded it they had turned inward, like a snake eating its own tail and consumed itself.

Beaupre Miller's body went unclaimed, he'd had no living relatives, when it was finally transferred to a processing plant. Cal joked that it was being turned into Soylent Green.

There were rumors that the war was winding down, not the first time these filtered in. Valentine would believe it when she saw it. Only a few days earlier in Egypt one of the pyramids had been blown up. No one took credit, not many bothered anymore and few Americans were going to shed tears over a pile of rocks.

Then a Sunday arrived, Cal and Valentine both had the day off so she packed a lunch and went to the park for a picnic. They arrived to find they had the place to themselves. Cal followed Valentine across the green and they spread their blanket next to the jungle gym. She kicked off her sandals before taking a seat beside him. While they lunched on cold chicken and potato salad, washed down with beer they spoke about many things, but neither brought up the future. There may be a life for them outside the Line, but they were no longer in a rush to get there. They still had their youth, money in the bank and time on their side.

After eating they lay down for a nap. Valentine had just placed her head on Cal's chest and was about to close her eyes when she heard it, a bird signing. She sat up, it took a few seconds of scanning the tree line before she located it, a wild canary perched into a tree. It had a black crown and wings, its breast a bright yellow. It continued to sing for another minute before it flew away, Valentine watched until it finally disappeared from her view.

She wished Cal could've seen it, but he'd already drifted off to sleep. Valentine silently thanked the little bird for its tiny gift, which she took as a blessing. She then laid down beside Cal, moments later she, too, was asleep, a smile on her face.

THE END

also by **Pete Trudgeon**

SUMMER of ANTOINETTE

Matthew Dante is a screenwriter living the idle, good life in Europe, After the tragic death of his family he's forced to return to America. Matthew sets about reacquainting himself with his childhood home. Almost immediately his life is altered the day he meets Antoinette Mouse, an alluring teenage girl, staying with her aunt over the summer. They begin a taboo affair that at times turns hallucinogenic and introduces him to the Bronze Peacock, a secret society dedicated to the worship of the nymph. As sinister forces threaten their relationship, he begins to suspect his love may be something more than just an ordinary girl.

DOT
SCREEN
STUDIOS